DESOLATION

ANGELS

THE BIG EMPTY Series

The Big Empty

Paradise City

Desolation Angels

No Exit

THE BIG EMPTY

DESOLATION ANGELS

BY
J.B. STEPHENS

razOr
bill
NEW YORK

The Big Empty 3: Desolation Angels

RAZORBILL

Published by the Penguin Group
Penguin Young Readers Group
345 Hudson Street, New York, New York 10014, U.S.A.
Penguin Group (USA) Inc., 375 Hudson Street, New York, New York 10014, U.S.A.
Penguin Books Canada Ltd, 10 Alcorn Avenue, Toronto, Ontario, Canada M4V 3B2
(a division of Pearson Penguin Canada, Inc.)
Penguin Books Ltd, 80 Strand, London WC2R 0RL, England
Penguin Ireland, 25 St Stephen's Green, Dublin 2, Ireland
(a division of Penguin Books Ltd)
Penguin Group (Australia), 250 Camberwell Road, Camberwell,
Victoria 3124, Australia (a division of Pearson Australia Group Pty Ltd)
Penguin Books India Pvt Ltd, 11 Community Centre, Panchsheel Park,
New Delhi – 110 017, India
Penguin Group (NZ), Cnr Airborne and Rosedale Roads, Albany,
Auckland 1310, New Zealand (a division of Pearson New Zealand Ltd)
Penguin Books (South Africa) (Pty) Ltd, 24 Sturdee Avenue, Rosebank,
Johannesburg 2196, South Africa

Penguin Books Ltd, Registered Offices: 80 Strand, London WC2R 0RL, England

10 9 8 7 6 5 4 3 2 1

Interior design by Christopher Grassi

Library of Congress Cataloging-in-Publication Data

Stephens, J. B.
  Desolation angels / by J.B. Stephens.
    p. cm. — (The Big Empty ; #3)
  Summary: After learning that the head of their community of Novo Mundum wants them
killed, five teenagers escape into the Big Empty—a lawless space left desolate after a
virus destroyed much of the human race.
  ISBN 1-59514-008-5 (pbk.)
  [1. Survival—Fiction. 2. Science fiction.] I. Title. II. Series:
Stephens, J. B. Big Empty ; 3.
  PZ7.S83214De 2004
  [Fic]—dc22

                                                            2004026069

Printed in the United States of America

ONE

LIZA HATED LYING TO MARIO. SHE HATED LIARS, NOW MORE than ever. But when the dark-haired guard had caught her sneaking around the compound at night, what choice did she have?

"I couldn't sleep, and I thought I'd find my dad here. He's always working late in the research center," Liza told the guard, noticing the shadows under his eyes, probably a product of working the night shift.

"Yeah, but I don't think your father is inside tonight. Last I saw, Dr. Slattery was over by the admin building. Your uncle's office," Mario said, causing a painful catch in Liza's chest. But now wasn't the right time to feel that, to feel anything. She had to focus.

Was Mario really not going to let her in? Was he just

going to send her back home? *Home.* Another word that carried whole new emotions for her. The home that once gave her comfort had become the last place she felt safe. Not while she was still lost in her own head, trying to sort out the twisted lies her father had spun. The dutiful father. The caring leader. The new savior of worthy, hardworking people.

It was all a lie, Liza knew that now, but she couldn't wrap her brain around the shattering ramifications of the pain her father had unleashed right here on the Novo Mundum campus. Designing a new, devastating strain of virus and testing it on human guinea pigs . . . an act so depraved she had vehemently denied that her father could have had any involvement until the facts slammed her in the face. Files. Case studies. Laboratory results. These past few years Daddy had been extremely busy in the research facility, and when she'd questioned him tonight, she'd realized that the noble light she'd seen in his eyes was far from benevolent. Her kind, caring father had fooled the world. *And I was the biggest fool of all.*

And now the word was *escape.* Michael was pushing everyone who could be trusted, telling them to gather supplies and find an escape route before their collusion was discovered—and before her Dad's new "experiments" or "security measures" killed someone else. At this moment Michael's friends were scouting ways out and foraging for supplies. Amber had promised to secrete some produce and dried grains, Irene medical supplies. Liza and Michael were supposed to be sneaking into the admin office to scan maps of the campus for possible ways out. Keely, more into strategy, had reeled off lists of items they would need in the Big Empty, the evacuated zone that surrounded this former college campus in the state they used to call Missouri.

Liza pulled her jacket tighter around her, wondering what it would be like out there. She'd lived on this campus long before the first outbreak of Strain 7, and though she'd seen news while it still existed, she knew the devastation of the real world was far worse than she'd imagined here in the safety of the compound.

Well, what she'd thought was safety . . .

She let her eyes flicker over the side of the building to the red maple trees, their branches swaying in the wind. Michael was hiding back there somewhere, waiting for Liza to gain entry into the lab, then signal him in through a window.

At the last minute she had persuaded Michael that they needed to visit the lab to search for true ammunition—a vaccine for the new strain of virus. If she and Michael's friends were going to leave, she wanted them armed with immunities from any illness her father could spread across the country.

Unfortunately, her most recent plan faced resistance with the folded arms of Mario, a teenage security guard.

"Can I just go in and look for him?" Liza asked, trying to keep the tone of desperation from her voice. Considering all the times she had cajoled and pushed past guards, she didn't know why she was suddenly so nervous, breaking a sweat under her hooded sweatshirt.

"I know his spots," she went on. "Where he goes to think, where he goes to sleep sometimes."

"I don't know." Mario screwed his mouth over to one side. Although she'd always found him a little dopey, with his long, dark ponytail and sloping posture, she felt a momentary flash of compassion for him. He was blindly trusting . . . just like she'd been.

"Oh, come on." She shoved her hands into her jeans pockets and dug her nails into her palms. *Please say yes,* she willed him.

"Yeah, okay." He cracked half a grin and stepped aside to let her pass.

Thanking him, Liza pressed on to the next obstacle, her brain filling with images she didn't want to consider. Like what waited for her in the Big Empty. She'd heard the stories from kids who'd traveled through it, the disgusting things they'd eaten to survive, the gruesome corpses they'd had to pass over.

Her sneakers squeaked over the tile floor, disturbing the eerie darkness. No time to fathom the horrors of the outside world. *Focus, Liza. Get Michael inside.*

TWO

Blackened, shriveled arms reached out to him. The stench of rotting flesh filled the air. Unseen mouths wailed in agony. They were getting closer . . . and closer . . . and . . .

"No!" Diego woke with a start. He raised his head off the dusty tarpaulin he'd passed out on and took in the dark, foreign shapes around him. Weak moonlight shone through rusted-out holes in the roof, allowing him to discern a stack of weather-beaten tennis rackets, an ossified ball shooter, and a few scattered tubular cans. A mound of netting lay heaped in the corner like a gigantic pile of drab spaghetti.

The equipment shed. Right. Irene had sneaked him out of the hospital lab and stashed him there while they figured out their next move and while Diego tried to will the medication out of his system. He was safe—for now.

Suddenly he heard a noise—a faint scuffling sound right outside the door.

Diego quickly jumped to his feet, wincing at the tightness in his thigh. He grabbed a length of corroded pipe and slunk back against the wall, trying to blend into the shadows.

"Diego?" came a familiar whisper. A shape moved toward him, liquid curves in the darkness.

"Irene," Diego rasped, setting down the pipe. "What the hell is going on?"

"I came to check on you. Make sure you were all right." She stepped forward into the dim light and Diego could see lines of worry crisscrossing her forehead.

"I'm fine." He raked the dark hair out of his eyes. No need to tell her about the nightmares and the pain in his bad leg from spending four hours on a cold concrete floor. "You just scared the crap out of me, dropping in here in the middle of the night."

"We're all sneaking around tonight. We've got to get out of Novo Mundum, fast. Apparently you weren't the only victim of the Slatterys." Irene leaned her head into his shoulder, her curls ticklish against his face. He wanted to close his arms around her waist, but he sensed her deep exhaustion and disappointment. Instead he put a hand over her shoulder and rubbed it gently.

"Escape? Let me lead the way."

"I'd be glad to, just as soon as we figure how to get out of here. Michael is on it, and we're all doing our parts, gathering supplies and looking for some route out of this prison. Michael is still freaked about the electric fence he helped install. Probably still thinking about what happened to Gabe."

Diego rubbed the back of his neck, trying to sort the murky details that Irene had passed on to him about the past week. Locator disks being inserted into the arms of Mundians. A high-voltage electric fence that had been activated without warning, killing one of the guards, Michael's friend Gabe. And then there were the human subjects of Dr. Slattery's experiments, desperate, moaning, dying patients whom Diego had discovered suffering inside the campus research center. Diego would have been scheduled to join them had it not been for intervention by Irene and Michael.

"It's all so crazy," she murmured. "When I think of what we went through to get here. You finally arrive in paradise and it bites you in the butt."

"No such thing as paradise." Although some kids called this place Paradise City, Diego never fell for the notion of utopia.

"I know that now. And somehow I've got to get this all across to my father without inciting a panic, and I know he's going to be devastated."

Diego paused, leery of spreading the word beyond their small, tight group. "Have you told your father and Aaron anything about what's going on yet?"

"I haven't seen them since it all unraveled, but I will. As soon as I get a chance."

"And"—Diego took a breath, trying to choose his

words carefully—"are you sure they'll believe you?"

Irene's eyes narrowed. "Of course they will."

Diego said nothing. He remembered their trek to Novo Mundum and how worried Irene had been after getting separated from her father and brother. She'd broken off from them to take care of Diego, who'd been hit by a soldier's bullet in the Big Empty. The way Diego saw it, he'd cost Irene her family once, and he had a bad feeling it was about to happen again. Mr. Margolis had staked too much on the perfect society of Novo Mundum to turn and abandon the place. But that was something Irene would have to discover herself.

"So when do we leave?" Diego said. "And how does Michael figure on doing it?"

"He's hoping we can sneak over the fence tomorrow night before it becomes electrified, but we need to make sure we have a safe path after what happened to Gabe. In the meantime we're all supposed to act normal and gather up as many supplies as we can without raising suspicion." She shook her head. "Act normal. Ha! Like that's even possible right now."

He turned his head toward her, noticing the sweet smell of her hair. "I can think of a few normal ways to pass the time." Easing back down onto the tarpaulin, he pulled her along.

"Hey!" She settled beside him with a laugh, then shifted so that she faced him, her hip bones jutting against his thighs, her pale face tipped up to the moonlight. The feel of her body against his sent forgotten sensations shooting through his nerves.

Slowly, as if pulled by her gravity, Diego leaned forward and pressed his mouth to hers, and she opened her lips, returning the kiss with warm emotion. His pain completely evaporated and the jagged remnants of his nightmare retreated from his mind. Once again Irene was just what he needed.

"It'll be okay," he murmured, gently trailing his fingers down her neck to the smooth collarbone, then venturing lower. She gasped as he cupped her breast, then pressed his mouth to hers in another deep, long kiss. The touch of her fingertips caressing his back, the way her hips moved against his . . . it was all driving him wild.

That was the thing about Irene, the way he could lose himself in her, the way she met him on his own level, unafraid, strong, and nurturing.

"I should go back," she whispered, pressing her lips into his neck. "I have to gather medical supplies before the early shift starts."

"No," he said softly, enclosing her in his arms, unwilling to let her go. Last night they had kissed for the first time, and he wasn't willing to let the growing heat between them die down. Not now. "Stay here with me."

She dug her fingers under his shirt. "Okay," she said, pressing against him. "Okay . . ."

THREE

WHAT THE HELL IS SLATTERY DOING IN THE LAB IN THE MIDDLE of the night? Michael thought as he pressed himself against the wall behind a row of thick polyurethane haz-mat suits. Liza stood beside him, gripping his arm.

They should never have come here. What a total waste of precious time. At first he'd been excited when they found Slattery's files on the vaccine for the very virus the scientist had been cultivating—until they read them and discovered there was no viable vaccine. Not yet. From what they could decipher, Dr. Slattery was still trying out possible antibodies in clinical trials—*human* trials. The same lab experiment Diego had been slated to take part in tomorrow.

He could still see the look of numb horror on Liza's face as she skimmed the entries, barely legible in her father's jagged scrawl. Then when they heard the footsteps and garbled voices echoing up the corridor, she'd turned even paler. Luckily she'd had the presence of mind to scramble into the equipment closet with him.

"What do you mean, there was a break-in?" came the deep, mellow voice he had recognized as Dr. Slattery's, growing louder and closer.

"One of my guards just reported it," came Frank Slattery's gruff, clipped tones. "Someone removed the boards from the south door."

Michael's hand tightened reflexively as he remembered yanking off the thick planks so he and Irene could rescue Diego from the lab. He had assumed it wouldn't be discovered till morning. Obviously he'd been wrong.

"It had to have happened within the last few hours," Frank went on. "Where the hell were you anyway? I checked all over."

"Liza asked to see me. I was talking with her when I heard you needed me."

Liza squeezed Michael's arm. After the shock she'd been through over the past few hours, it was amazing she wasn't a basket case. He just hoped she could keep it together until he got her out of this hellhole.

"Liza wanted to see you? This late?" Frank asked, sounding concerned. "What's wrong?"

"She's upset," Dr. Slattery replied. "She blames you

for Gabe's death. Told me she was in the office and saw what you were doing. She thinks you electrified the fence."

"Jesus, Paul. I hope you told her she misunderstood it. Or that it was a mistake. Tell her it was new technology and I didn't know what I was doing."

"I tried, but you know how she is. Persistent. Inquisitive. And her boyfriend was friends with the kid that got killed."

"The boyfriend is a liability," Frank said flatly. "It's too bad he wasn't taken out along with his friend."

Rage flashed through Michael at the mention of his friend. Not that he hadn't been sure that Frank had killed Gabe, but hearing him admit it was almost unbearable. It took all his self-control to remain hidden in the damned closet.

"Now, let's take it easy," Dr. Slattery said, a little testily. "We're not in the business of taking lives."

Frank snorted. "Do you hear yourself?"

"Loud and clear." Dr. Slattery lifted his chin. "I do what I must to protect our community. That's what it's all about, isn't it? Protection? We arm ourselves against invasion, against future viruses, against fear itself. That's what we're about, Frank. Don't ever lose sight of it."

It was one of the most deluded, twisted explanations for killing that Michael had ever heard, though he imagined it might be similar to a military creed, the justification for killing to protect other lives.

"I just have to ask, did you lure those soldiers here

on purpose?" Dr. Slattery asked. "Was this all about getting that electrified fence?"

"Don't start up about that again," Frank barked. "Thanks to that fence, I was able to save you from a potential setback. It will protect us. It will protect all of Novo Mundum."

"It's an unnecessary drain on our resources, and it's distracting you from your other duties, this break-in being a perfect example. Someone has been snooping around the lab and getting away with it because you focused your time and manpower setting up that fence."

There was a long pause, and Michael was aware of the tension between the brothers. But when Frank spoke again, there was no hint of his usual gruffness. Instead he sounded contrite.

"You're right, Paul. I know securing Novo Mundum is top priority for both of us, but you and I come at it from different angles. Anyway, it won't happen again. The fence is almost up and the electric grid should be operational in the next twenty-four hours."

In the next twenty-four hours? A cold sensation spilled through Michael's chest. He'd been hoping to sneak out of there as soon as nightfall came again, counting on the fact that the fence would still be offline. Now it might be on again.

He turned to Liza and mouthed: *Now what?*

She shook her head, her eyes distant as she focused on the continuing conversation between the two men, as if she could figure things out by studiously following along.

Michael couldn't believe her patience, her strength, after all she'd been through. And on top of that, she was preparing to leave her father, this place that had insulated her life while the rest of the world had suffered a global plague. He couldn't help wondering how much longer her calm demeanor would hold.

FOUR

KEELY CEMENTED A LOOK OF DISTRACTION ON HER FACE AND leaned over her desk to rest her chin on her left hand. With her right hand, she hastily slipped the handful of protein bars into the open backpack at her feet.

Stealing from children. It had actually gotten this bad.

She wouldn't dare raid the classroom if she had any other option, but there was no choice. She and her friends needed to gather as many supplies as they could before slipping through an unfinished part of the fence tonight—only twelve or fourteen hours from now. And for most of those hours she had to be right here at her post or risk raising suspicion.

Still, she was glad of the chance to see her students

one last time. She stared out at them now, trying to memorize each child's face. Splotches of morning sun dappled their hair as they bent over their books and papers during their morning quiet time. Some were reading, some daydreaming. Olivia was doodling away on a scavenged piece of cardboard, her freckled face scrunched in concentration.

Keely hated to leave them behind in this place, now that she knew its deep dark secrets. But she wouldn't be any help to them dead—or crippled by a fatal new virus strain. She could only hope she would get to safety and then figure out a way to rescue them.

Pretending to scratch her leg, she quickly pulled a box of Band-Aids out of her lower drawer and dropped it into the pack. *Let's see . . . snack cakes, flashlight, compass, bandages . . .* she thought, making a mental tally. *What else?* Her eyes roved around the room until they spied a teetering pile of mats in the east corner. Once nap time was over, she would roll up a couple of those and stuff them in her pack. They could probably use them as bedrolls.

But enough theft for now. Keely kicked her pack into a shadowy corner beneath her desk and got to her feet. As she strolled down the aisle, pausing to check on each child's work, her mind raced ahead. She didn't look forward to returning to the Big Empty, a wasteland of displaced malcontents, reactionary gangs, and misguided soldiers. She forced herself not to think about that, to focus for now on their escape. Michael was all about eluding the new security system he'd helped install on the campus, but Keely was more concerned about the logistics of actually getting out. This campus had been built on a peninsula, accessible by a main road that had been taken out with explosives, to discourage visitors. The remaining ditches had become filled in with rocks and water, making passage treacherous at best. There was access over the lake by boat, but the beach was well guarded, as were the short supply of watercraft.

It had been difficult getting in. Getting out seemed nearly impossible.

She paused beside Olivia, who was scribbling furiously with a piece of pink chalk, filling in the center of the fat heart she'd drawn.

"Miss Gilmore?" Olivia asked without looking up. "Do you have a boyfriend?"

Something sharp and heavy pressed against Keely's chest. And here she'd been doing a pretty good job *not* thinking about Gabe.

Gabe. It still hurt so much. She hadn't realized what a presence he was in her life until he was gone. She already missed his rakish smile and caustic sense of humor, even his groan-inducing come-ons. And whether she'd let herself realize it or not at the time, there was also that faint hope he'd given her that one day she could be with someone again.

He hadn't been her boyfriend—not like Eric. But for the first time since Eric, she'd let someone halfway in. She and Gabe had bonded during their mission to retrieve the GPS disks in St. Louis. They'd saved each other's lives and returned here triumphant only for him to die. It was horribly ironic and tragic . . . and so freaking unfair. Not that unfair was anything new for Keely.

"No, Olivia," Keely replied, trying to push all traces of grief from her voice. "I don't have a boyfriend."

She should have known this place was too good to be true. It probably would have been better if she'd never come to Novo Mundum. Maybe if she'd stayed in L.A. with her shell-shocked mother, she wouldn't be pilfering food and bedding from kids. Maybe Amber and the others would have found a different, safer place to escape to. And maybe—her throat suddenly constricted and her vision blurred—*maybe Gabe would still be alive?*

"Excuse me."

Keely's head snapped up at the sound of the deep male voice. A guard was standing in the classroom doorway—older, bigger, and more intimidating looking than most of the lanky teens who worked security. Olivia instinctively pressed against Keely.

"Keely Gilmore?" he said flatly.

She sucked in her breath. "Y-yes. I'm Keely Gilmore," she said, straightening up, trying to appear strong and calm in front of the children.

The guard gestured into the corridor. "I need you to come with me."

"Uh . . . I really can't do that," she said, clasping her hands behind her back to prevent them from shaking. "I'm in the middle of a lesson right now."

"It won't take long. One of the other teachers

has offered to watch the class while you're gone."

Keely looked past him and saw Bela standing in the corridor, shrugging at her.

"I don't understand," Keely said, turning her attention back to the guard. "What is this all about?"

"I was asked to bring you to the clinic. Dr. Slattery is making sure key personnel have their GPS disks inserted. You were scheduled for this morning."

Keely felt a prick of dread. *Right. But I figured I'd blow it off since I don't need a pesky disk to track my escape.* But when she'd skipped the appointment, she hadn't expected a personal escort to the clinic.

"How about if I head over after class?" Keely suggested lightly.

"How about right now," the guard said firmly, clamping a hand around her wrist with alarming strength and determination.

They're afraid of me, she realized. Slattery knew she had info on him. That was why they took out Gabe. Now they were targeting her, even at the risk of alarming her students and any other Mundians who happened to see her being dragged across the campus.

"Okay," Keely said, realizing there was no point in resisting as she stepped out into the stark autumn sunlight. *You can stick a locator device in me, make things more difficult, but you can't own me. Not now or ever.*

FIVE

SWAB, SLICE, JAB, BANDAGE. SWAB, SLICE, JAB, BANDAGE. Repeat thirty-something times.

That had been the extent of Irene's morning. In the past two days she'd honed expert skills inserting the GPS disks, but she still hated the process, and her mouth actually ached from forcing a smile.

The eagerness of people here really killed her, the way they enthusiastically rolled up their sleeves. Then once they were bandaged and given their disk numbers, they would thank Irene as if she'd done them a huge favor. Which made her feel that much guiltier.

"There you go," Irene said, adhering a bandage to the arm of a tall woman with black, crescent-shaped eyeglasses.

"This thing won't hurt me . . . right?" the woman asked, poking the flesh around the bandage.

Irene hesitated. This was the first person to actually show any uneasiness about the disk. "It shouldn't. But if you see any signs of infection, let us know right away."

"Okay. Well, thanks."

There was that word again. Irene felt a stab of guilt. "Not a worry," she forced out, biting back the urge to grimace at the irony of using Novo Mundum's seriously untrue credo.

"Irene?"

Irene glanced over and saw her father and brother, Aaron, coming down the hall.

"Dad? What are you doing here?" She pulled off her latex gloves and threw her arms around him in a tight hug. With her face pressed to his shoulder, she shut her eyes and basked in his familiar strong embrace. "Hey, Aaron," she added as she pulled back, lifting her hand in a wave.

"Hey." Her brother hung back slightly, thumbs hooked through the loops of his faded carpenter pants.

"You must be exhausted," her father began, shaking his head in dismay. "I can't believe you're still here after working all night."

Irene could feel her cheeks grow hot as images of her body entwined with Diego's unspooled in her mind. "Well, you know . . ." she said, fiddling with her smock. "There's a lot to do right now." How could she explain that she'd been too busy to head home, too busy stealing files with evidence of Slattery's experiments, breaking Diego out of the research facility before he could become a human lab rat? That she'd been planning an escape from Novo Mundum? And that she'd spent the night with her outcast boyfriend?

"Irene?" Nurse Chong leaned in between them, hugging a stack of files to her chest. "Please don't stay away from the table too long. There are still quite a few people waiting and we have a large group coming in this afternoon."

"I'll just be a minute," Irene replied.

Nurse Chong nodded, then bent her head to the endless paperwork at a nearby counter.

Irene's father scanned the line of people waiting for their disks. "Have you been doing this all day? Aren't you going to get a break?" He spoke loud enough that Nurse Chong would be sure to overhear.

"Sure, I will. Don't worry about me. What are you guys doing here?"

"We leave for guide training in an hour and wanted to say good-bye."

Irene gasped. "Today? But I thought you weren't going till the end of the week."

"That was the plan, but the weather seems to be changing fast, so they moved it up a few days."

"But you can't leave. Not yet." Irene's stomach tightened. If they left today, they would miss the escape. She had to stop them. She had to tell them everything she knew right now and pray that they could figure a way out of their trip so they could escape with her.

But how could she? There was no way she could

untangle the whole sordid, snarled mess for them—not now, and definitely not here, with Nurse Chong watching from a few feet away.

There was only one clear, simple, *horrible* answer: she would have to leave without them.

"What do you mean?" Her father's thick brows scrolled together. "Why can't we leave now?"

"Because . . ." She stalled, switching to an alternate plan. She couldn't stop them, but maybe they'd be better off not knowing the truth for now and better off at least being somewhere other than here. "I can't let you go without some extra emergency supplies. Let me find some for you."

She scurried around the corner into a nearby workroom and grabbed a handful of Band-Aids, a small tester tube of antibacterial cream, a tiny vial of expired aspirin. Then she picked up a nearby pencil and scrawled a message on one bandage wrapper.

Remember Santa Fe in May.

It would have to do. Her father had always wanted to go to Santa Fe. When Strain 7 hit, they had been planning a ski vacation there. She could only hope he would find the note later, guess at its meaning, and devise a way to meet her there in six months.

Pasting what she hoped was a casual expression on her face, she clutched the supplies to her chest and stepped back into the hall. "Here you go," she whispered, shoving the bandages and vials into her father's coat pocket. "Don't let Nurse Chong see. We're not supposed to play favorites."

"Thanks, sweetie," her father said. "Now we really should get going."

Irene grabbed his arm, suddenly overcome by an intense fear that she would never see him again. "Please be careful," she said. "And . . . I love you."

Her father smiled. "Love you too, hon. And don't worry. We'll be fine. Right, Aaron?"

"Right." Aaron lifted one side of his mouth in a cool-dude-type smile. "Not a worry."

It killed her to hear her older brother recite the vernacular of this place so readily. "Bye," she said hoarsely.

"We'll see you in a couple of weeks." Her father gave her a quick kiss on the cheek and walked away.

Irene watched them head out the door, their figures darkening to silhouettes as they hit the bright sunshine. Tears stung her eyes, but she took a deep breath, forced them back, and, robot-like, trudged over to the waiting area.

"Next?"

SIX

KEELY'S MIND WHIRLED AS SHE WAITED INSIDE THE MUSTY room of the clinic. She was intensely aware of the guard standing outside the door, and her forearm ached where the bullet had grazed it two nights ago. To think that she'd risked her life to bring back those damn disks. She had felt so proud, so . . . *heroic.* And now they were going to force a locator disk inside her, allowing them to track her every move.

A man in a white coat poked his head in. "I'll be right with you," he said in a bland voice, "soon as I work through the line outside." His eyes seemed vacant, disaffected.

Maybe that was what happened to health care workers in the post–Strain 7 world. After being on the front lines during all that dying, their instincts and training worthless, maybe they had to turn a little cold in order to get through it.

Keely felt a familiar ache as she remembered her mother's blank stares and zombielike personality. Maybe she'd been too hard on her mom. After all, Keely never really knew what she had to go through day after day.

Of course, her mother never bothered to *tell* her either. Keely had always thought she worked triage at the local hospital, but one of the higher-ups here at Novo Mundum had hinted that Mom had been lying all along, that her mother was actually working for the government, doing biochemical research.

Secrets. Everyone had them. Both Mom and Novo Mundum. Somehow, though, her mother's deceitfulness cut Keely the deepest.

"Okay, then, you need a disk?" Irene appeared in the doorway, her dark curls tossed behind the elastic of a surgical mask.

Keely gasped, happy to see those familiar dark eyes, even if they were looking a little bloodshot. "That's why I'm here," she said, gesturing toward the guard outside. "By special invitation."

Irene stepped into the small room and pulled latex gloves from the box on the wall. "Don't worry," she said, her eyes steady. "This won't take long. I'll just shut the door."

Yes! Keely thought. *Shut the door and we'll figure a way around this.*

"Not a good idea." The heavyset guard appeared suddenly in the doorway. "Let's just leave it open."

"Okay." Irene turned away from him and bent over Keely's arm. "You need to roll up your sleeve," she said, loud enough for the guard to hear.

Keely did so, noticing the guard peering in the doorway over Irene's shoulder. "This alcohol will feel cool," Irene said as she carefully swabbed a section of Keely's skin. The guard's eyes were on them as Irene took the tip of the scalpel and made a small, quick incision on Keely's upper arm. He wasn't going to let anything slip on his watch.

"Ouch!" Keely said, but not from the sting of the blade as much as for the guard to hear. He frowned, as if he'd seen enough, then stepped away.

"I need your other hand right here, to keep your sleeve out of the way," Irene instructed. She lifted Keely's right hand and positioned it palm up beneath the incision.

"Um . . . sure," Keely said nervously.

Irene picked up a large pair of tweezers and grasped the tiny, pill-shaped GPS disk. Then she leaned far forward, blocking Keely from the open door. "Okay, now hold still . . ." she instructed.

Keely looked away, gazing up at the dusty ceiling tiles instead. All of a sudden something small and round plopped into her outstretched hand.

The GPS disk.

"All done," Irene said. "That wasn't so bad, was it?"

"No." Sagging with relief, Keely lowered her hand and deposited the GPS disk in her jacket pocket. It would be one less problem once they made it out of this place. "Not bad at all."

SEVEN

"I'M TOO PREGNANT FOR THIS," AMBER GRUMBLED AS SHE tramped through the wet layer of detritus carpeting the grove of trees. She was only in her fifth month. So why did she feel so bloated and enormous, as if every step required supreme effort?

The first gardening shift had ended and all the other workers were carrying bags and boxes of harvested food to the meal preparers—something they didn't allow Amber to do because of her condition. Now was the perfect time to raid the storage shed. *If* she could get her ass in gear.

She paused to catch her breath, bracing herself against a spruce tree, and ran the back of her hand over her forehead.

Yuck. How could she be all sweaty when it was chilly today?

Because I'm learning how to walk all over again, she answered herself. *Because this little bugger inside me is throwing off my center of gravity.* She just hoped she didn't slow everyone down when they left Novo Mundum and headed into the Big Empty. Escape. Damn. Just thinking about it made her feel all shaky. The last thing she wanted to do was trek across the Big Empty. It wasn't that she was scared—at least not for herself. But that was the thing. She couldn't make the decision simply for herself anymore. She'd be putting Peanut in harm's way too.

She pushed off from the tree and continued lumbering toward the storage house, more sideways waddle than forward motion.

Hard to believe that just twelve hours earlier she'd been in a blissful sleep—snoring, most likely. Those were two pregnancy side effects she hadn't known about: deep, sound sleep with vivid, full-color dreams that should come with popcorn and Milk Duds. And the ability to snore like a wild boar.

Then Keely had woken her with all the bad news, telling her how they had to gather supplies all day today in order to be ready to bail. It sounded like a bad dream.

If only.

Deep down she had always known Novo Mundum was too good to be true. It was just in her nature to doubt anything good that came her way. People did crappy things to other people; she'd learned that the hard way. And no matter how everyone tried to pretend this was some perfect "Kumbaya"-singing society, it was still just a bunch of people. It made sense there'd be a few assholes in the bunch. It was just too bad they ran the place.

The storage house finally loomed into view. The campus fire station in its former life, the long cinderblock building was basically one giant garage, with a few other rooms attached. The food growers used it to store grains, canned foods, seed supplies—anything with a shelf life longer than a couple of weeks.

Amber was just heading toward the entrance when a movement through the trees caught her eye. On the other side of the clearing were two Mundian guards, rifles at the ready. They were peering inside an old Dumpster that was now resting on its side, skirted by tall weeds.

Why the hell are they looking in that thing?

She stepped back into the cover of the trees. Better they not see her, but if they did, she could just tell them she was checking inventory. There was no rule against her being in that part of the campus. And it wasn't like she was wanted for some sort of crime.

Suddenly a weird prickly feeling crawled down Amber's back. Of course. She knew exactly what the guards were doing: searching for Diego. She remembered Keely telling her that Michael and Irene managed to break him out of the lab and hide him in the old tennis shed. All the more reason for them to escape as soon as possible.

Novo Mundum wasn't a very big place. It wouldn't take long for them to check every conceivable hiding spot.

The guards finished poking around the Dumpster and continued south toward the library. As soon as they were gone, Amber toddled to the door of the storage house and opened it with her key.

Inside the smells were overwhelming, making Amber's head reel. Yet another perk of pregnancy: a nose like a bloodhound. She quickly opened up her bag and began filling it with homemade protein bars, dehydrated fruit and vegetables, and a few rare strips of dried meat, holding her breath as she worked. By the time she had filled her bag, a dull throbbing had started up behind her temples.

This was irony at its worst. How could a pregnant woman be sickened by a pile of food? Maybe she'd eaten something bad last night.

Amber fastened her pack and pulled it on, taking a moment to steady herself under the added weight. Then she walked out the door and took a deep breath of fresh forest air.

She was just about to start on the road toward her dorm when she heard the voices. It was Starsky and Hutch again. They had doubled back and were now rooting around a clump of bushes—right along the path she needed to take.

Amber muttered a string of curse words. Just what she needed. What if the two idiots decided to search for Diego in her backpack? Now she would have to take the long way back.

Before they had a chance to see her, she cut through the trees and headed east, venturing into the more overgrown part of Novo Mundum. There were no buildings this way, just a dense pocket of oaks that shaded the gardens. It was less likely the search parties would concentrate on that area.

The light was dimmer under the trees, and again her walking was hampered by the thick carpet of leaves, grass, and moss that had built up over the last couple of years. Before Strain 7 she'd never realized how quickly Mother Nature could take a place over. With no more mowing, raking, or trimming, parts of the old campus now resembled a lost Mayan city, a group of ramshackle structures poking out from beneath vines and fallen twigs.

Once again she was dripping with sweat and her breath was coming in ragged gasps. She really needed to sit, but where?

And then she saw it. Up ahead in the distance stood a large, round tree stump. It was the perfect place to park her butt for a couple of minutes—her own little oasis in the woods. Except for all the bird crap. And the rancid smell.

Amber trudged toward it, wheezing as she went. As she neared the trunk, the stale, mildewy scent grew even stronger. *Yuck!* What was that anyway? Had something curled up and died? Just her luck to stumble onto a squirrel graveyard with her new, superhuman smelling skills.

Coming closer, she could see it wasn't a tree stump

at all but the old storm drain, built to draw rainwater through the hill toward the lagoon. Her boss had pointed it out on her first tour of the grounds. The growers fed all the runoff irrigation into it so there wouldn't be any stagnant water breeding diseases in Novo Mundum.

She shuffled forward and plopped down on its rusted metal lid. Smelly or not, it was still a good place to sit. As long as she didn't break the thing and fall through.

Just then a new, prickly sensation swept over her. Snatches of thoughts strung themselves together. The drain. . . It ran downhill to the lake . . . *under* the electric fence.

That was it! Their way out of Novo Mundum!

Amber's breathing quickened. She had to tell the others. *Come on,* she commanded herself. *Move your fat butt.*

Gathering all her strength, she forced herself up onto her feet. But the sudden motion made her head reel and her stomach capsize. Before she could prepare herself, her body doubled over and she lost her lunch.

Uck. *That* didn't help the smell problem.

Come on. Come on. All she had to do was get to the garden path and into some fresh air. She could see it up ahead, just beyond those two trees. Or was it four trees? She couldn't tell. If they would just stop wiggling . . .

Shit! she thought as the world slowly tilted sideways and grew dark. *I can't pass out! I can't. . . .*

EIGHT

Shouldering her bag of stolen goods, Keely pushed open the door to her dorm room, eager to tell Amber about the "save" Irene had pulled off at the clinic today. "Amber?" she called as she walked through the door. "You here?"

No answer.

Keely peeked into the bathroom, where Amber spent more and more time these days. "Amber?"

It was empty.

A sudden coldness spread through her. Amber wasn't there. In fact, it looked like she hadn't been back yet at all. This was bad. No note, no signs of life.

What if she got caught?

Keely quickly stashed her bag underneath her bed

and ran back outside, racing in the direction of the food storage unit. Screw looking carefree. If Bree wasn't back yet, something had already gone wrong.

Amber, she corrected herself. *Not Bree.*

The first time she'd seen Amber in the New Orleans train station, Keely had been reminded of her younger sister. They were close to the same age, same build, similar coloring. But that was where the similarities ended. Amber didn't have Bree's sweet disposition or easy smile. She was streetwise and obnoxious. Still, sometimes Keely would watch her sleeping, and she seemed so vulnerable and innocent. It was almost like having Bree back again. Except for the snoring.

Keely finally reached the storage house and yanked on the door. It was locked tight. She pressed her head against the glass and cupped her hands around her eyes. From what she could see, the place looked dark and empty. Had Amber even been here yet? Could she have been held up at the gardens?

Only one way to find out.

She whirled around to leave and ran smack into a zippered parka. Keely jumped back, screaming, and saw that the parka was attached to a tall, Mundian guard. Another one stood behind him, hands resting on the rifle slung around his neck.

Stay calm, she told herself. *You haven't done anything wrong.*

"What are you doing here?" the closest one asked, his voice kind but concerned.

"Oh, I—I was just curious," she stammered.

"Thought I'd explore the old firehouse, but it's locked."

"It isn't a firehouse anymore," the guy explained. "They use it for food storage. That's why it's locked."

"Oh." She nodded solemnly. "Are you guys protecting it?"

"No. We're searching the grounds for . . ." He paused, as if catching himself in an error. "We're out patrolling."

She knew exactly what they were up to—hunting for Diego. Keely wondered if they were the reason Amber wasn't home yet. Maybe she hadn't been able to get in the storage house with them poking about.

"Well, thanks," she said in her most serene Novo Mundum voice.

"Not a worry," said the taller of the two guards.

They lifted their hands in a farewell gesture and headed toward the main road, grumbling to each other.

"Are we supposed to get a dinner break?"

"Not until the next shift relieves us."

"Crap. Too bad they didn't give us a key to that food house."

Keely waited until they were quite a ways off and then charged through the trees toward the gardens. The branches were thick and she felt a sharp twig scrape the skin of her forehead. Damn. She didn't think of that before. Amber probably would have had a tough time making it through this brush in her condition.

A low groaning sound startled her, too low to be a bird and too high to be an animal. Keely followed the noise until she saw a mound of color through the trees.

Amber! She was lying on her side, moaning. Her pack lay nearby, a couple of protein bars scattered on the ground beside it.

"Amber?" Keely said, racing over. She bent down and gently grasped her shoulder. "Amber it's me, Keely."

Amber's lashes fluttered slightly; she was alive but weak.

Oh God. Something was really wrong. Amber's skin was the color of mayonnaise and her face was so swollen, she barely even resembled herself.

Keely kicked the pack of food beneath a pile of leaves—they could come back for it later—and knelt down beside Amber. "Don't worry," she said. "It's going to be all right." She slid her arms underneath Amber's shoulders and, slowly and carefully, pulled her backward through the brush toward civilization and help.

NINE

THROUGH A HAZE OF PAIN AMBER HEARD THEM TALKING about her.

High blood pressure . . . the baby . . . swelling . . .

Her head hurt, her feet and hands throbbed, and she felt disconnected from reality. Her eyes were too heavy to open, but she could hear the concern in the doctor's voice. For the first time Amber wondered if there was something wrong with her.

"The baby?" she croaked.

"Don't worry, Amber." Someone touched Amber's shoulder, and she felt herself drifting away again, away from the pain. In her mind she was opening a door, a hatch in a field. Inside was a water slide, a looping, splashing thrill ride that shot water right over the fence of Novo Mundum.

The drain. She had found a way out. She had to tell her friends. Forcing her eyes open, she tried to focus. Irene stood over her, and someone was squeezing her hand. Keely?

"She's waking up," Keely said.

"How are you feeling, Amber?" Dr. MacTavish asked.

Amber tried to answer, but her body wasn't up to responding.

"Why don't you see if she can drink some water?" the doctor suggested.

Keely pressed a straw to her lips and Amber was able to suck in cool water.

"The baby's heartbeat sounds normal, but your blood pressure is dangerously high," Dr. MacTavish said. "I can't be entirely sure with these caveman facilities, but the hypertension, the swelling, and the fainting lead me to believe you've developed something called preeclampsia."

Even though she didn't know what that meant, the verdict hit Amber like a stone.

"What is that?" Keely asked.

"It's a common condition for pregnant girls her age," Dr. MacTavish explained. "I won't lie; it can be serious, because it brings a risk of blood clots and seizures. But we can monitor it and hopefully prevent that from happening. She'll have to take it easy and remain on bed rest for the rest of her pregnancy."

Bed rest? That wasn't going to work. Not now. Not when she'd finally figured out their escape. Amber glanced up at Keely's stricken face, then over at Irene's sympathetic one. *Help me here,* she pleaded silently.

"Is that really necessary?" Irene asked. "I mean, if she takes things slow, she'll be okay, right?"

The doctor frowned. "No guarantees."

"We're serious about this," Keely told the doctor, looking toward the door. She lowered her voice. "We're trying to get Amber out of here, but it's going to be a long trip. Long and unpredictable."

Wait—what was Keely doing, saying that to Dr. MacTavish? Amber blinked, then remembered Keely telling her that among all the other insane things that had happened the night before, the doctor had discovered the truth as well and was pretty much on their side.

"And I'm telling you all seriously, it's highly unlikely that Amber could survive a trip like that right now," Dr. MacTavish said. "It'll probably kill her. The baby too. I'm sorry, but there's no way she can take on intense physical activity in her condition."

"But . . ." Amber managed a word of protest, then fell silent, placing her hands on her belly. As much as she wanted to leave, there was no way she could hurt Peanut.

"Now if you'll excuse me," Dr. MacTavish said, heading for the door, "I'll let you guys plot without me. There are some other people waiting for my special bedside manner." She fixed Amber with a final, fleeting look—as close to a kind expression as Amber had seen on the doctor—and then disappeared into the noise of the lobby.

"You're going to be okay, Amber," Keely said as the door shut again. "And we'll come back for you as soon as we can. You can probably make the trip once the baby is born."

Amber shook her head. "But I can't go with you guys now. I'm going to be stuck here. Alone."

"Maybe not," Irene said. "So far we haven't found a way out through that fence. We might be here longer than you think."

"Nope. I found it," Amber rasped. "I've got the answer. I know the way out."

TEN

JONAH LOOKED AT HIS FINGERNAILS. THEY WERE STILL FILTHY, even after a good scrubbing. He wasn't surprised, considering he'd spent seven hours straight dismantling unneeded machinery so that Ridley could use the scrap for the new fence. He'd probably retain the aroma of WD-40 for the rest of the week.

As he moved through the food line, his eyes kept roving around the cafeteria, inspecting each face, searching for one with long dark curls and doe-like eyes. Unfortunately, Irene wasn't there.

Jonah hadn't been able to stop thinking about her all day. He really hoped she was all right. Their run-in the night before had left him feeling profoundly sad. He hated to see her risk everything for Diego. She had so much to offer Novo Mundum, and Diego, although a great guy, was just never going to make it.

But he had to admit, that was one of the things he loved about her. She cared about people—probably too much.

"Hi there," said the first server in the food line, a pretty, college-age girl with short brown hair and pixie features. "Want some cracked sunflower bread?"

"Sure," Jonah replied, returning her wide smile. "Thanks."

"Not a worry." She nodded at him and placed a couple of slices of bread on his tray. Jonah could hear her enthusiastically greet the next person as he moved on to get his soup.

That's how it should be, he thought as he grabbed a bowl of barley-and-vegetable stew. *We should treat everyone equally and look out for the whole group— not waste ourselves on one or two.*

He had just taken a seat near the corner when a shadow loomed over his table.

"Hey, Jonah, my friend."

Michael.

Jonah eyed him warily. "Got a problem, man?"

"I heard the fence is finished," Michael said, lowering his voice. "That the electric grid will be online this evening."

"Yeah." Jonah spooned up some soup, but Michael bent down, pushing into Jonah's face.

"Jonah . . . it can't happen. The grid has to stay down, just for one night. Is there any way you could do that? Make sure it doesn't work?"

Jonah gritted his teeth. "Sorry. Don't think I can."

"I'm not asking for anything permanent," Michael added quickly. "Just something that will buy us enough time."

To escape, Jonah thought, mentally finishing Michael's sentence. He remembered how they were trying to make Dr. Slattery out to be some Dr. Frankenstein. But how could they jump to such conclusions? They weren't scientists. His virus research was probably designed to protect Novo Mundum and its inhabitants. Okay, so maybe he was using real people as test subjects, but they were probably like Diego, too weak to survive. What was the big deal if they were going to die anyway? If Jonah knew he didn't have long to live, he'd gladly let Dr. Slattery experiment on him in order to help others. After all that man had done for them, he deserved the benefit of the doubt.

"It's not that easy and you know it," Jonah said. He wished Michael would leave—just run off and try to get someone else to do his bidding in that patented Michael way of winning people over. Because it wasn't going to work on him. Michael might have been the pseudo-leader when they were trying to find their way to Novo Mundum. But as far as Jonah was concerned, that ended the minute they arrived. "In fact, we shouldn't even be seen together right now," he added, meeting Michael's eyes. "Maybe you should move to the next table."

Michael didn't leave. "Jonah, *please.*"

"Give it up, Michael."

Jonah noticed a few people eyeing them curiously. It was clear he and Michael were having a disagreement—something rare in public at Novo Mundum.

Jonah picked up his bread and pushed away from the table. He hated to waste good soup like that, but he had to get away from Michael.

He stepped out into the sharp November sunshine and stalked down the cracked sidewalk that led to the cafeteria courtyard.

"Jonah! Wait!"

Damn! Michael had followed. Jonah's fist clenched around the bread slices, crumbling them slightly.

"Look, I'm sorry," Michael said, jogging up beside him, "but you really are our only hope. I know you have access to certain systems that could throw the fence off-line. All I need is for you to toss a tiny wrench into it. Make it look like a malfunction."

Jonah shook his head. "Why won't you just lay off? Why can't you realize that I *can't?*"

"Because you can!" Michael hissed. "If you want to stay here, fine, but don't you care about us? About Keely? About *Irene?*"

A flash of rage coursed through Jonah. Michael had some balls, acting like Jonah didn't care. Jonah had been a team player, a good friend to everyone in that group. But they were on a different track now, a losing track. And Jonah needed to cut loose. Self-preservation.

"Don't give me the sob story, Michael," Jonah said impatiently. "You've got it great here. I don't feel sorry for you at all."

"Great?" Michael snarled. "Great isn't when your best friend is electrocuted. Gabe's death is on *me*, Jonah. *My* fault." He thumped his chest. "I can't let that happen again."

Looking at Michael's shattered expression, Jonah felt a tinge of pity. "Sorry, but count me out. You all really need to rethink this. You know what it's like out there." He nodded in the direction of the forest. "It's not worth it."

Michael stared down at his shoes. "You don't understand," he said in an unsteady whisper. "You just don't get it."

"Michael! Jonah!" called a distant voice.

Irene jogged toward them down the curved road, her cheeks flushed with the cold. Jonah felt his heart skip around his rib cage. It was strange how he could have her image memorized to the last detail and still be blown away by her each time she came near.

She paused when she reached them, catching her breath. "It's Amber," she gasped. "She's in the hospital."

"What? What happened?" Michael demanded.

"She's had a complication with her pregnancy. It's serious, but they know how to help her." She leaned forward and lowered her voice to a faint hum. "But there's no way she can do anything . . . strenuous." Her eyes widened with hidden meaning.

Again Michael seemed to shrivel with guilt. "That may not matter," he mumbled. "I can't find us a safe way out."

Irene grabbed Michael's arm. "But that's something else I came to tell you," she said excitedly. "We've found a way."

Color returned to Michael's face. "Really?"

Jonah felt a sudden rush of anxiety. They were going. *She* was going. He'd tried his best to warn them—to stop them—but it hadn't worked.

"Tell me," Michael insisted quietly. "What is it?"

"Wait," Jonah cut them off. "I don't want to hear it."

They eyed him in silence.

"You know I'm not going," he said. "And I know you're all making a stupid mistake. A huge mistake. But I can't stop you."

"Jonah—" Irene began, but he held up a hand to shush her.

"I don't want to know what you're planning," he explained. "I'll keep quiet, but don't make me lie for you."

Irene stared at him for a moment, then nodded sadly. "Okay."

Jonah stood there awkwardly, wondering how to end it. These people had been his friends—still were, really—but he'd probably never see them again. That realization left him feeling hollow inside.

Irene reached over and gave him a tight hug. "Take care of Amber," she whispered. "And yourself."

He didn't want to let go, but suddenly she was sliding out of his arms. Jonah stole one last look at Irene, then walked away without looking back. How could a girl so smart go back to the desolation out there? He just didn't get it.

In here they had everything to live for, and out there . . .

Out there in the Big Empty, there was nothing worthwhile.

ELEVEN

MORNING CAN'T COME SOON ENOUGH, LIZA THOUGHT AS SHE watched Michael inventory the meager weapons she'd managed to swipe from the emergency shelter set up for her father. There were a hunting bow, a quiver, a pack of titanium-tipped arrows, and a set of bowie knives, and though Michael seemed pleased with the stash, the more he talked about their escape route, the more she just wanted it all to be over.

"Great," he said, testing the string of the bow. "This stuff will definitely come in handy. Diego's an expert hunter. Just try to wrap things watertight when you pack. We want to keep things dry in the drain."

"A storm drain?" She was a strong swimmer, but the idea of floating through a pipe was a little scary.

"Amber found one that passes far under the fence," Michael explained, his eyes narrowing. "We slip in and ride the tide to freedom."

Freedom. Michael and me. A feeble smile played across Liza's face. As frightening and unreal as everything was, she could at least find comfort in one superseding fact: she would be going through this with Michael. She knew it would be rough going, but this would be *their* escape—the start of *their* life together.

Ironic, how Liza had always envied his relationship with Keely, a closeness formed out of their journey to Novo Mundum and their mission to retrieve the disks. She'd wanted to go on that mission with Michael but had never expected they'd be thrown together this way, never expected to lose so much in the process.

A scuffle at the door brought her out of her thoughts, and Michael mouthed the words, *Who is it?*

"Must be my father," she whispered, motioning Michael toward the closet. He gathered the stolen weapons and ducked away as her father called out to her. She crossed to the door and opened it.

"Hi, honey."

"Daddy . . ." She hadn't laid eyes him since the night before, and now it was surreal, almost as if she were staring at a stranger. Here was the person she had loved and trusted all her life, the center of her world after Mom died, and now being so near him triggered intense hatred inside her.

Liar. Fake. Monster. She would never forget the

things he'd said in the lab. That cavalier tone of voice as he'd dismissed her feelings. She would not let him control her. Not now. Not ever again.

"Feeling any better today?" he asked, sitting in the chair next to her bed. "You were so upset last night."

Act normal. Be cool.

"Yeah," Liza mumbled, sinking onto her mattress. She hesitated a moment, wondering what to say. It made no sense to keep accusing Uncle Frank now that she knew for sure her father was in on it too. "I guess you were right that I just needed some sleep to clear my head. I do feel better."

"Well, I want you to know that I looked into the issue regarding your uncle," he said, resting his elbows on his knees and steepling his hands. "I didn't tell Frank, but I had some people check things out, and one of the engineers brought up the possibility of a power surge. You know how we're always patching systems together, stealing power from one facility to light another? And sometimes we think something is shut down, but there could still be some lingering power. That seems to be what happened to that young man."

Gabe, Liza wanted to shout. *He had a name.*

Her father rose and began pacing her narrow room, shaking his head as if riddled with remorse. Liza tried to remain calm as he drifted past the closet again and again.

"When a tragedy like this happens, we demand answers," he continued. "But we have to realize there may not be any. Sometimes what we think we see— what we think is right—is not really true at all."

A faint hope shimmered inside her. Could he be trying to tell her something? She gazed into his deep-set blue eyes, feeling confusion spread through her. Maybe all the evidence they'd found against him was wrong. Maybe he really *was* doing something innately good. What if they could get it all straight, solve everything right now, clear his name, and end this whole nightmare once and for all? Then she could pick up her dreams for the future right where she left them off. She would still be with Michael but here in Novo Mundum, where it was safe, where she had a family. . . .

"Liza, honey," her father continued, his voice somber. "If your uncle discovered he was responsible for that young man's death, even accidentally, it would eat him up." He paused and stared out the window at the gathering storm clouds. "But . . . if you want me to investigate further, I will."

"I don't know. . . ." Everything was so confusing, so overwhelming. She struggled to grasp a concrete thought. "It's not about persecuting anyone," she said. She closed her eyes, trying to recall exactly what she'd seen in the office that moment.

"Of course not. That's not what we're about. Safety is our major concern, and that's one of the things I wanted to tell you myself. In fact, I just finished an autopsy on Gabe, and I found something curious."

"What do you mean?" She turned toward him, surprised.

"There were some signs of distress unrelated to the

accident." He paused, as if searching for the strength to continue. "Signs of an infection."

"An *infection?*"

He nodded. "We think Gabe, Michael, and Keely might have been exposed to a pathogen while out on their mission. It's vital that we get Michael and Keely into quarantine as soon as possible."

"*What?*" Liza sprang up from her bed, staring at him in horror. Quarantine? No. *No!* It was bullshit. He just wanted Michael out of the way.

It was like bursting out of a cocoon. Liza suddenly realized that this was how her father always operated. He led people down a path of his choosing, only he made it seem like it was all their idea. Had she always been so easy?

"Don't worry. It's just a precaution. And I'm sure you weren't exposed." He stood, bracing her by the shoulders. "I just wanted you to know that you might not be seeing Michael for a while."

Again she stared into his familiar blue eyes—eyes she'd always thought so worthy of trust and admiration. Not anymore. It was like seeing him with super-sharp vision for the first time in her life, as if some new prescription—a heavy dose of reality?—was revealing his true form. Now his gaze struck her as cold, focused inward rather than outward; his voice sounded slick and his movements seemed expertly choreographed.

Her father really was a monster. And to think she'd considered trusting him again! She was *such* an idiot.

But she wouldn't let her rage show. She had to continue playing the part.

"Oh my God!" she said slowly. "Poor Michael. I hope he's going to be all right." It wasn't hard to cry.

"He will," her father consoled. "He's strong. In the meantime you are not to see him. Understand? It's for his safety as well as your own."

She nodded bravely and yessed him over and over again as he told her to take care, to rest up, not to worry too much. By the time she heard his footfalls heading down the stairs, she was roiling in anger.

She opened the closet. "Did you hear that?"

"Every freakin' word." Michael stepped out, his eyes wide in disbelief. "I'm on your old man's hit list. And we can forget about leaving in the morning." She swung around, their eyes locking as he picked up a backpack from the floor of the closet. "We have to leave tonight."

TWELVE

IRENE SHOOK THE RAIN OUT OF HER HAIR AND STEPPED INTO the murky darkness of the old college "English house" that had become the home she, Aaron, and her dad shared with two other families. For some reason, the front room felt colder tonight, maybe because she knew Dad and Aaron were gone.

She sank into a chair and dug into her pockets, emptying them of the medical supplies she'd swiped, until she finally pulled out a halfway hardened slice of sunflower loaf wrapped in a cloth napkin. She turned the bread over in her hands, staring at it blankly, and then suddenly the tears were falling freely as all the fear and frustration she'd managed to bottle up during the day spilled over. Escaping Novo Mundum was hard enough to comprehend, but now she'd be leaving without Amber, Jonah . . . *Aaron and Dad.*

She grabbed the back of the chair and sobbed.

This wasn't like her. She had to pull herself together. She couldn't waste time feeling sorry for herself. She had to finish gathering up the rest of her supplies and wrap them in plastic for their escape through the drainpipe. Once they were safe, she could go over all this in her head. At least Diego would be there to help her.

A sudden pounding on the door made her jump. Michael? Keely? Whoever it was, it sounded urgent. Irene hastily wiped her face and pulled open the door.

"Irene Margolis?"

"Yes?" she replied, blinking to focus. In the dim light she could see the shadowy figure of a latex suit.

"May I help you?" she asked nervously.

"You need to come with me," he said brusquely.

Icy prickles skittered down her spine. "Why? What's wrong?"

"You've been ordered into quarantine."

"Quarantine?" It didn't make any sense. "I don't understand. For what?"

"You were exposed to a dangerous virus while working on the patient Gabe Vickers. You know the rules . . . quarantine."

She shook her head. "Gabe didn't die from a virus. He was electrocuted."

"Apparently he was a carrier and you were exposed while preparing the corpse."

Irene took a step backward. This was insane. "But I

took precautions. Besides, I barely worked on him. I couldn't have been exposed."

"Dr. Slattery himself did the autopsy, and he believes you were."

Of course . . . Dr. Slattery had ordered this. There was no exposure—just a ruse to pull Irene into isolation, out of circulation in Novo Mundum. Someone must have figured out her connection to Keely and Michael and Diego, realized that she knew too much about the secret workings of this place.

Irene knew there was no use resisting; this guard was only doing his job. But as she followed him out the door, she wondered frantically if she could find some way to elude him and make a break. Once in quarantine, she would never get out alive.

The rain was picking up as they continued down the road and into a patch of darkness beneath some trees. Irene could only make out varying degrees of blackness and the hazy border of the road up ahead.

Suddenly she heard the rustle of branches and the pounding of footsteps. She turned in time to see a large shadow swoop down out of nowhere, followed by a muffled groan. Then something large and heavy fell at her feet.

"Irene?"

It was Michael's voice. A flashlight clicked on, revealing Michael, Liza, and Keely standing over the sprawled form of the guard.

"Are you okay?" Keely asked. "We saw that guy taking you out of your building. Did Slattery send him?"

Irene nodded, still too stunned for speech.

Michael stepped over the guard. "They're coming for us, all of us," he said, taking a backpack from Liza. "It's time to get out of here."

THIRTEEN

"THIS MUST BE IT. JUST LIKE AMBER DESCRIBED," KEELY announced as they approached a dark mound in the hill behind the campus greenhouses.

This is really it, Liza thought. She was leaving Novo Mundum. She knew it was the only choice, but fear and cold, driving rain had worn away the initial thrill, and she couldn't stop worrying about what it was like inside this dark, underground pipe.

"I'm telling you, do it now. Take this damned thing out," Michael told Irene. He had been arguing with her about removing his GPS disk throughout their trip across the campus. "Take it out before we go down there. If Frank and his cronies turn on that program, the person at the computer is going to see exactly where I am. Like a lighted beacon to guide their way right to us."

"I can't cut you open just as we're going into a sewer pipe," Irene argued. "Do you know what the chances of infection would be?"

"I don't give a crap about infection right now," Michael said.

"And we don't have time," Diego interceded. "Look, let it go for now, and Irene will take it out when we've moved on some."

"Can we get this thing open now?" Keely asked, chancing a brief beam of the flashlight on the drain cover. In the darkness and rain the sewer cap looked just like a tree trunk; the light revealed a rusted man-hole cover on top.

Distracted from his argument, Michael pried it open with a stick and slid the cover to the side. "We'd better take it one at a time," he said.

"I'll go first," Diego said, hitching himself up onto the cement-skirted mound.

"Wait," Liza said quickly. "Do we really know what's down there or where it leads? What if the pipe is clogged? If we get trapped down there under water and mud, I mean . . ." She swallowed, trying to keep the tremor out of her voice. She didn't want Michael's friends to think she was chicken, but she did think they should minimize their risks.

"The drain is clear." Diego straddled the side. "If there was a clog, there'd be backup from the rain we had last week," he said, lowering himself down the ladder.

"And right now this drain is our only option," Keely added, climbing up behind Diego.

"Though I could do without the smell," Irene called as she followed them down.

Suddenly it was just Michael and her. "Go on," he said. "I'll come in after you."

She approached the mound and looked down. Yep. It was a big dark hole all right. Somehow she hadn't imagined it to be so dark and narrow, and she wasn't prepared for the smell, more rot than oxygen.

Liza held her breath as she gingerly climbed down the rusted ladder. The temperature immediately dropped as she descended, and there was a faint whistle of wind through the large pipe. As she neared the bottom, the beam from Keely's flashlight illuminated a small shape at the foot of the ladder.

"A dead raccoon," Diego said, his voice echoing off the walls. Keely and Irene stooped next to him, covering their noses. "It must have gotten washed down in here during the last round of heavy rains."

"What else could be down here?" Keely asked.

"Field rats. Maybe snakes," Diego replied calmly. "But don't think about that."

Liza carefully stepped over the raccoon corpse and hunched up against Keely, pressing herself against the wall to make room for Michael. The sides of the pipe were freezing cold and the cramped conditions were starting to get to her.

Overhead, Michael balanced himself on the ladder and slowly slid the manhole cover back in place, closing out all light from the rainy night sky. *This is insane,* Liza thought. *We could be trapped in here, and no one would ever find us.*

"We need to move fast," Michael said as he stepped off the ladder. "The rain is picking up, and we don't want to be stuck in here if it floods."

Diego crouched near the mouth of the tunnel. "Give me the flashlight. I'll go first." Tucking the flashlight in the collar of his coat, he got down on his hands and knees and crawled into the pipe. Keely went next, followed by Irene.

Liza was next in line. Her heart drummed so loud in her ears, she barely heard Michael say: "It's okay. I'm right behind you."

Adjusting her pack, she got down on her knees and pressed her hands down into the slimy silt that coated the bottom of the pipe. Then she headed into the tunnel, following the weak, amber-colored light up ahead.

Almost immediately the walls narrowed. Liza fought off the panic, bracing herself with each splash through the muck. *You can do this,* she told herself.

The floor sloped gradually downward and she could feel water rushing down around her. What if it pooled up at the bottom? "Michael?" she said shakily.

"Keep going," came his voice from behind. "Just keep going as fast as you can."

She waded forward, keeping her eyes on Irene's silhouette. *Think of sunny days on the lake,* she told herself. *Remember the smell of wildflowers and honeysuckle. Think of anything but this place, this moment.*

Suddenly she bumped into Irene. "We have to stop," Irene called back.

"What's going on?" Liza called.

"We're stuck," came Keely's distant voice.

Stuck? Icy panic gripped her. Without the steady forward motion she was too aware of her dire surroundings. The darkness. The sour smell. And the freezing water that was now halfway up her forearms.

"What do you mean, stuck?" she called.

Diego shouted some things she couldn't hear. Then word traveled back. "There's a shift in the pipe up ahead and the mud has built up, blocking the way," Irene explained. "Diego and Keely are trying to dig through."

We're trapped. Liza sat back on her feet and rubbed her cold hands against her jacket. *Just breathe.* She shut her eyes, trying to imagine herself somewhere else, but this time it was no use. The water was rising fast, washing over her hips.

She turned to Michael's dark outline. "What do we do? Should we go back?"

He didn't reply.

"Michael, say something!"

"I don't know," he said. "I just . . . don't know."

A shout came from up ahead.

"They've got it!" Irene called over her shoulder. "We're moving!"

Liza lowered her head and pushed on. The water was up to her elbows, its swift current helping to push her forward. An object brushed against her and continued downstream. Liza thought of the dead raccoon and shuddered.

The tunnel seemed endless, and Liza felt a new rush of panic. What if there was no end to it? What if the rainwater rushed in too fast, trapping them all? She lifted her chin against the rising water, which now sloshed up to her shoulders.

More shouts sounded up ahead, followed by total, utter darkness. Liza froze. Where did the flashlight go?

Again Irene gave the message. "Diego said we're going to have to swim underwater the rest of the way."

"But we'll drown!" Liza cried, sputtering as briny water splashed into her mouth.

"No!" Irene yelled back. "He said it shouldn't be far. Just ride the current and don't panic." She splashed forward, then shouted, "Okay, I'm going!"

"Irene?" Liza called. But she was already gone. "Oh God. Oh no, no, no."

Michael touched the back of her head, just above her pack. "It's all right," he said. "Just take a deep breath and go. When you hit the lake, swim as hard as you can."

He was right. She had to go. Already the water was splashing into her nose and mouth, choking her, and it was exhausting having to strain against the force of the current pushing her forward.

Liza lifted her mouth to the small pocket of air, took a deep breath, and plunged into the swirling darkness.

The flow was fast and strong, slamming her against the pipe walls and tugging fiercely at the pack on her back. Just when panic was about to take over, Liza was shot forward into dim light and roaring noise. Then her body hit the hard expanse of the lake.

Bubbles roiled around her, and she struggled to swim up, up. . . . At last her head broke the surface of the lake. Gasping for breath, she treaded water and tried to get her bearings. A hard rain pelted the surface of the water, and the world felt enormously wide after their trek through the tunnel.

Suddenly Michael emerged a few feet away, coughing and spluttering. "You okay?" he croaked.

Liza fanned her arms through the cold water, glad to be free of the dank, dark pipe. "I think so."

"Swim over that way," he said, gesturing toward the shore of the lake, where Liza could make out the others.

Soon her hand hit the gravelly bottom, and she pulled herself up and waded through the heavy water. As she plopped onto the shore, exhausted but relieved to be breathing, Diego was taking inventory and rallying them to move on.

Move on . . . Liza could barely lift her head, but she knew Diego was right. They needed to keep moving. Away from Novo Mundum. Without a word, Michael helped her to her feet, and she struggled up in her wet clothes. She could go on. She had to. Besides, with Michael there, she could handle anything.

FOURTEEN

MICHAEL STARED THROUGH THE DRIZZLE INTO THE DARK, ominous countryside—their new home for who knew how long. His clothes were still wet, half frozen stiff with cold. Only his surging adrenaline kept him thawed enough to keep moving.

So they escaped. So what? Escaped back to the Big Empty . . . from one hell to another.

The way he saw it, the past few months essentially boiled down to this: He and his friends struggled through the dangers of the Big Empty to get into a place that, unknown to them, was run by two madmen. Soon after he arrived, Michael rose in their favor by bringing the big bosses technology that made them even more treacherous; then he finally wised up in time to bust himself and his friends out of there. Now they were back at square one, traipsing through the wilderness with danger all around. Really the only thing they'd gained was one more set of people to run from.

Then again, he'd also found Liza.

Michael studied her profile as she trudged through the trees, her stride long and cautious, arms out as if trying to balance herself on a high wire. What the hell was he thinking, bringing her along? At the time he'd thought he was helping her, but now he wasn't so sure. Of course she'd said she wanted to come, but she didn't have any idea what it was like out here, and he could tell she was scared.

Now he would be responsible for her—just like Maggie and all the others. And he'd failed all of them. Liza was looking to him to guide her, but how could he when he didn't trust himself to make the right decisions anymore?

If there was one thing he'd always been good at, it was reading people. He'd prided himself on it. It was like he'd inherited a super-concentrated form of his father's salesman genes. Just by talking casually with people, he could instinctively size them up, assessing their moods, their fears, what he could get away with and what he couldn't. It had served him especially well in post–Strain 7 New York. But Novo Mundum somehow stripped him of that power. How could he have been so wrong about Dr. Slattery and Frank and even Dr. MacTavish? Bad suddenly became good and good became hellishly evil. It had cost Michael his confidence, but it had cost Gabe his life.

The group continued trudging up and down endless hills, past scattered houses with boarded-up or smashed windows and farms that looked like they'd been abandoned for fifty years instead of one or two. The sounds of their collective footsteps and breathing formed an odd, discordant symphony. As they crested a slope and headed onto flatter ground, Irene turned from her spot near the front of their line. "I think we should stop," she called out. "We need to get out of these wet clothes."

"Not yet," Diego said without turning his head. "Got to keep moving, and I know this terrain. We're in Missouri, just north of the area I grew up in. We should get some distance between us and Novo Mundum while we can navigate the area."

"Distance won't save us if we all get hypothermia," Irene countered.

"It's not that cold," Diego insisted. "I've been out in worse. Besides, we might get more hard rain. No point in getting two sets of clothes wet."

"Diego, everyone is tired and you're limping." Irene turned to the rest of them, folding her arms across her chest. "A little support here? Michael, don't you think it's time for a break?"

"No," Diego cut in. "We need to move now while they still think we're in Novo Mundum." He turned and looked at Michael. "Right?"

Michael pressed against the disk in his arm, wondering if Frank was tracking their moves at this very moment. He wanted to stop and cut the thing out, but he didn't want to argue with Diego, didn't want to make the decisions. Not anymore.

But the others walked alongside him, waiting for an answer.

"I don't know. Whatever Diego says," he replied with a sloppy wave.

"But—" Irene began.

"I don't know!" Michael snapped.

The silence that followed was loaded with tension. Then Diego said, "Okay, let's go." And they trod on.

Michael gritted his teeth. Let them listen to Diego for a change. He was bound to do a better job than Michael ever could.

A hand grasped his arm. Liza's eyes were wide with concern under her rain-slicked hair. "Are you okay?" she asked.

"I'm fine," he said, with a little more snap than he'd intended.

"It's going to be all right."

Michael felt a flash of annoyance. "You don't know that. You don't know what it's like out here in the Big Empty."

Liza lowered her chin to her chest as she trudged on. "I know it's got to be better than Novo Mundum."

He paused as the guilt flooded back, diluting his anger. "Look," he said, pulling her aside and letting the others pass. "I'm sorry. I should have prepared you for this."

"For what?"

"We aren't out of danger yet. We may never be. You'd

be a hell of a lot safer back in your father's kingdom."

Her eyes flashed in the darkness. "What are you saying? That I shouldn't have come? That I can't cut it out here?"

"No. I just . . ." He felt his jaw clench in anger. "I just don't think you realize how hard it's going to be."

"And I don't think *you* realize how hard it would be to go back."

Michael watched as she marched on, her oversized pack bouncing on her back. Of course she couldn't go back. And filling her with panic wouldn't help her face whatever lay ahead. "You're right," he said. "I'm sorry. I'm just . . . not myself."

Liza stared down at the ground in front of her feet. "And I need you to be Michael. Now more than ever."

Again he felt the weight of her hopes, of everyone's hopes, piled on his shoulders.

"I'll try." He reached for her hand, rubbed it for warmth, then twined his fingers through hers. When she squeezed back, he felt a twinge of hope as they walked side by side into the woods, into the darkness.

FIFTEEN

"WAKE UP, DALTON." A GRUFF MALE VOICE PIERCED JONAH'S dreams.

He stirred slightly, floating gradually into the present.

"Dalton, get up," the voice commanded again. A heavy hand clasped his shoulder and shook it vigorously.

Jonah opened his eyes and saw Frank's head silhouetted against a bright lantern. "Mr. Slattery?" he said, sitting up and blinking against the light. "What's wrong, sir?"

Frank backed up and sank into a chair, his rough features suddenly illuminated by the lantern on the table. Fear swept through Jonah, erasing all residue of sleep.

Jonah had always been halfway scared of Frank. The man was large and loud, pronouncing everything in a booming bark. Plus he'd been cursed with a face that looked like it had been carved from ground meat, with its bumpy contours and pink, pockmarked complexion. But now, in the yellow light, Jonah could read a level of emotion he hadn't thought Frank was capable of expressing. His eyes were narrow and steely, his forehead rutted with . . . what? Worry? Rage? Jonah couldn't pin it down.

"There's been a breakout," Frank blurted suddenly.

Jonah blinked, guarding his reaction. "From where?" he asked, thinking of Diego and the lab.

"From here! Novo Mundum!" Frank snapped.

Jonah nodded. It was still a strange notion to him that anyone would want to escape *from* this place. Especially considering the hardships everyone had to endure to get here. People escaped from prisons or kidnappings—not from a sanctuary.

"Who was it?" he asked, sinking back against the bed.

"So you know nothing about this?" Frank lifted his chin, staring at Jonah through thin slits.

"No, sir." Listening to himself, Jonah realized he sounded completely natural. He really *was* surprised his friends had gotten out safely. Thank God he'd avoided hearing the plan. "What happened?"

Frank grunted as if satisfied with what he saw in Jonah. "Your friends, the ones you came here with from Clearwater—they've escaped."

Jonah let his jaw drop open. "But . . . how? Why?"

"We don't know yet. I was hoping you could tell me."

"Are you sure they're gone? Maybe they're just hiding somewhere around here. What about tracking their GPS disks?"

Frank stood and walked to the window, staring out into the black void beyond. "Only two of them had disks—Keely and Michael. Apparently Keely cut hers out and tossed it. Ended up leading half my men on a wild-goose chase. Bishop's readouts showed him already on the other side of the perimeter fence. Damn if I know how. Last we checked, he was on the far side of the lake, almost four miles out, heading north. The others must be with him."

"Damn," Jonah muttered, thinking of Irene and the others out in the wild, purposefully throwing themselves in danger. What a waste.

"I know," Frank went on. "And that's not all of it. We think Liza went too."

"Liza?"

"Dr. Slattery's daughter. We can't find her anywhere." Frank turned away from the window. "That damned Bishop. Who knows what he told her."

Frank's posture wilted slightly and Jonah caught a glimpse of someone else, as if a facade had been pulled away to reveal a stooped, sixty-something-year-old man. He suddenly realized what emotion he had been reading in Frank's face—pain.

"I'm sorry," Jonah said. "Is there anything I can do?"

Frank looked at him, his features relaxing in a pseudo-smile. "Actually, there is."

SIXTEEN

WITH HIS FACE JUST INCHES FROM THE SODDEN, DECAYED leaves of the forest floor, Diego inhaled the familiar scent of home and shifted his sitting position to stretch out his good leg. His eyes skimmed the dense brush of the sloping hill across the ridge, on guard, searching for movement. They'd been walking for hours—through the night—and though he could have kept going, he conceded to taking a break. The others had needed food and rest, and there was also the problem of that GPS disk in Michael's arm. Although Diego didn't credit the uneven technology of the staff at Novo Mundum, he agreed it was best to cut the thing out once and for all. Meanwhile the others rested on the closed-in porch of an old fishing house behind him, eating the rabbits he'd caught and skinned. The house was their second choice for a stop, the first one being a hunting lodge on the hill, but the sight of two corpses there had forced them to move on.

A crosscurrent of air carried the unmistakable scent of roasted meat. Luckily the breeze off the rushing stream and the dense crop of trees would filter and dilute the smell. Someone would have to be within several yards to pick up the scent—and by then Diego would be able to see them. Irene had offered to bring him some of the meat, but he'd refused. He needed to keep his hands on his weapon. And besides, he was fine just sitting there among the trees the way he used to do every day of his life.

After the confinement of Novo Mundum, Diego sucked up his freedom like a camel that had just found water in the desert. He could feel himself fully inhabit his body again, reclaiming senses and reflexes that had become stunted over the long, idle weeks. When he thought about what happened back in that so-called utopia and what they tried to do to him . . . Diego's hand tightened on the bowstring. He almost hoped a search party did catch up with them—*almost.*

The wind picked up slightly, rustling through the pine and cottonwood trees. Birds twittered, congregating on the lower branches, and the air was spiked with ozone. Looked like they'd be getting some bad winter weather soon.

Diego caught another whiff of the meat and his saliva glands kicked into gear. He imagined the rabbits must be done by now. He'd fashioned a low spit over a pit of burning moss and lichen. It took longer with such a low flame, but they couldn't risk burning anything that would create a plume of smoke. Besides, there was nothing tastier than rabbit slow-roasted in the open air.

Twigs snapped behind him. He turned and saw Michael climbing the hill, rolling down his left sleeve.

"Irene took that disk out?" Diego asked.

Michael nodded. "I threw it in the river along with the rabbit innards. Let the assholes chase carp." He stopped in front of Diego. "Let me take over while you eat."

Diego frowned. Not that he didn't trust Michael, but lately the guy seemed like a hollow version of himself.

"Naw, I'm all right," he told Michael. "You should rest some more."

Michael settled onto the ground beside Diego. "I'm done with rest. Just want to be alone for a minute. Go on."

Diego rose, testing his injured leg. Stiff, but not painful. "Okay. Let me know if you see anything suspicious on the horizon."

Down the slope in their makeshift camp, Keely and Liza leaned over a map as they picked the last of the meat from some bones. Irene looked up from the circle of watery morning light, where she was wiping down a scalpel with a cloth that smelled of rubbing alcohol.

"We saved you one of the rabbits," Liza said, "and Irene says it's probably safe to use the water here. It was rusty at first but tastes okay. Want some?"

"Sure," Diego said, taking a spot beside Irene, who handed him a piece of roasted rabbit.

"How's your leg?" she asked.

"Little stiff, but not a problem. How's it looking on that map, Keely?"

Keely traced a line on the map with one finger. "By my guess, we've already covered more than twenty miles."

Diego nodded as he bit into a charred rabbit leg.

"We were just talking about possible plans," Keely said.

"Like, where the hell we should go?" Diego asked.

Liza returned and handed him a plastic cup of water. "As far away from Novo Mundum as possible," she said emphatically.

A wounded look crept over Irene's features. "I hate to abandon the place completely. What about Amber and my dad and Aaron? Couldn't we stay on the fringes of Novo Mundum for a while? Maybe there's a way to get them out."

"Too risky," Keely said.

Diego was glad he didn't have to be the bad guy here. "Besides," he added, "you passed the old man that note, right? At least that gives you a shot at hooking up with him in the future. Right now we've got to get the hell away from that place. You know they'll be sending a search party after us. Since we have Liza with us, I'm half surprised they haven't run us down already."

Liza lifted her chin defiantly but didn't argue with him. Everyone knew it: the girl was shark bait. But that didn't mean she didn't deserve a shot at escape like the rest of them, and so far she'd been a pretty good sport, hiking along without a complaint. At the moment she was digging through her backpack, taking out rolled-up T-shirts.

"What's our goal?" Keely said. "So far we've been heading north."

"I know this area in every direction," Diego said. "I grew up here." He wished he could return to Nonnie's small farmhouse, where he'd holed up alone for months, but he knew it was no good. Last time he was there, the place had been crawling with soldiers. Including the one nervous G.I. Joe who'd shot him in the leg.

"If we go south, we'll hit occupied territory," Irene said. "But even if we keep up this superhuman rate of traveling, it'll take us a long time to walk that far."

"Weeks," Keely said, smoothing the map. "And that doesn't account for any of the hazards in between, like soldiers or crazies."

Diego wiped the edge of his mouth with his sleeve. "If Jonah came along, he might be able to rig up a car or truck for us."

Keely shook her head. "I think a train might be the answer. One of those ghost trains that bring supplies across the Big Empty. Amber and I hopped one once, and it worked for us. The thing is, we need to find one of their way stations, a train yard where they refuel and exchange cars."

"North," Diego said. "Outside St. Louis. But it'll still be a few days of hiking from here."

"And then what?" Irene asked. "I still have trouble with turning our backs on Novo Mundum. I mean, a lot of good people are there, people who deserve to survive what's going on there."

"And I can't go back," Liza said, looking up from a pile of clothes. "I'm serious. If you go back, Michael and I will have to split off."

"But what if Slattery sends his Strain 8 out in the world?" Irene asked. "I just can't walk away without trying to stop him."

Strain 8, the new virus that had almost been tested on Diego himself. The thought of Slattery injecting innocent "subjects" made Diego's blood go cold. Granted, the man had to be stopped, but there'd been no way to battle the king in his own empire. "We'll get there, Irene," he said, slipping an arm around her shoulders and pulling her close. "It's just going to have to be a later stage of the plan—after escape and survival in the Big Empty."

"So it's agreed, then?" Keely asked. "We'll head toward the St. Louis train depot. Get a train out of the Big Empty. Try to enlist the right people to stop Slattery."

Diego wasn't thrilled about trading the Big Empty for the Occupied Zone, but what the hell.

Irene tipped her face up toward Diego. "Don't you want to ask Michael what he thinks?"

"We can ask," Diego said. "But right now I don't think Michael is in decision-making mode."

"I'll run it by him as soon as I get this stuff reorganized," Liza said, taking another mound of clothes out of her pack.

"What're you doing there, Liza?" Keely asked.

"Trying to repack," she answered. "Things keep poking me in the back when we're hiking."

Noticing the silver butt of a pistol, Diego reached into the mound of clothes and picked it up. "Where'd you get this?"

"It was my grandfather's," she said. "And Michael told me to grab any weapons I could find."

Diego pointed it at the window, checking the weight of it in his hand. "In my experience, a gun is a dangerous thing when you don't know how to use it. There's a serious kick and it can misfire. Some guns send the casings flying, and they can burn the hell out of your hand. Besides, do you really have the balls to shoot someone?"

Liza's eyes flickered with something he couldn't define. Resentment? Or just fear? "I don't know for sure," she admitted.

He had to give her credit, bonus points for honesty.

"Why don't you give this to Michael for now? It'll lighten your load."

"You could take it," Liza offered.

But Diego wanted Michael to have the gun, wanted to share the arms. "I've got my longbow."

She shrugged, not concerned, though he could see Irene watching with disdain. "I hope you'll never have to use that," Irene said.

"That'd be nice," Diego said, thinking of the dangers of the Big Empty: renegade gangs like the Slash, families of rebels who'd die to defend their land, soldiers, and now any trackers sent out by Novo Mundum.

Although the "civilization" of the Occupied Zone seemed safe by comparison, that territory came with its own problems.

But that was where they were headed, right? Talk about a flawed plan.

SEVENTEEN

SNOW.

Once or twice Michael had seen snow in New York as early as November. But who would expect it here in Missouri or Mississippi or wherever the hell they were? He'd left that part of the trip up to Keely, who was all over the maps, but wherever they were, it was south, right? So why the hell did it look like Alaska out here?

At first it had been a nice diversion. A few fat flakes drifted down intermittently, salting the landscape and quieting the forest. Then the air was filled with white and a stinging cold set in. Now they all trudged in gloomy silence, their heads bowed slightly, their cheeks and noses the color of raw salmon.

Diego hiked in front, leading them along the side of

the riverbed so that they didn't make tracks. Irene walked directly behind him, followed by Keely and Liza. Michael took up the rear, which was fine by him. He didn't want the others to see the difficulty he was having.

A seam on his left boot had popped, separating the leather from the sole. As he walked, snow seeped through the opening. At first it just felt wet, then cold, then numb. Now thousands of tiny, razor-sharp icicles seemed to pierce his left foot every time he set it down.

But it was pointless to complain. What could they do? Not like there were any shoe stores in the neighborhood. Not likely there'd be any in the next five hundred miles of this wasteland.

"There's a lot of cover here. Let's stop and have a quick rest," Diego said as they reached the canopy of a large oak tree overhanging the river.

The group huddled together beside the bluff. Irene pulled out a canteen of water and started passing it around while Diego consulted the compass Keely had brought along.

Michael wedged between two of the tree's gigantic exposed roots, shuddering inside his jacket. The temperature seemed to be falling steadily and the cold knifed right through him. He decided to layer on the extra sweater he'd packed.

He unzipped his pack and searched through the layers of gear, right down to the bottom of the bag, but there was no sign of it. *What the hell?* he thought. Where was that sweater?

"Here, have a drink." Liza stood before him, holding out the canteen. She wore a scarf she'd fashioned out of a crocheted piece of cloth found in a house they'd used for a few hours. And poking out of her jacket sleeve was the cuffed end of his charcoal gray sweater.

"You're wearing my sweater?" he asked.

Liza lowered her arm slightly, staring at the woven material poking out at the wrist. "Well, yeah. I thought you said I had to stay warm."

"But where are *your* warm clothes?"

"I couldn't bring my winter stuff. All my sweaters were in my father's closet. I didn't want him to notice they were missing."

"So you just helped yourself to mine?" he asked. "What the hell did you bring?"

Liza stared at him as if she didn't recognize him. "Lots of T-shirts and stuff."

Michael's hands clenched. There was something about her answer that made his irritation boil over. Ignoring the shooting pain in his leg, he stomped over to her pack and opened it.

Liza followed. "Michael, I'm sorry," she said in a wobbly voice. "I thought you wouldn't mind. You seemed so worried before when I was cold, so I just put it on when we stopped by the river."

By now everyone was staring at him. Michael ignored them and kept rummaging through the backpack. Suddenly his hands hit on a large metal object. It was a handheld mirror—an antique, judging by the tarnished, ornate silver frame. "What's this for?"

Liza's face turned bright red. "It was my mother's," she said raspily. "I wanted to bring something of hers with me. To remember her."

Michael met her rumpled expression with disdain. "So you brought *this*?" he asked, lifting the mirror. "Why not pack a toaster while you're at it? An old MP3 player?"

"Michael . . ." Irene interrupted.

"This isn't just about you, you know," he continued barking at Liza. "Why do you always have to do this? Why are you always so selfish, Maggie?"

Everyone fell silent.

Keely grabbed the sleeve of his jacket. "This is Liza, Michael. Not Maggie."

Liza's face went ghostly white under the crocheted scarf, but she didn't turn away.

Michael felt himself crumble inside. Humiliation, followed by another flash of anger—this time at himself.

"Liza," he whispered. "I . . . I'm . . ." But the words died in his throat. Maybe it was better this way. He'd pushed some distance between them. She would be better off without him.

Diego took the mirror from Michael's grasp. "This is nice," he said to Liza. Reaching into the neck of his coat, he lifted out a gold chain with a crucifix. "This was my nonnie's," he explained. "It brings me strength. I'll keep it forever." He tucked the pendant back into his coat and bent over her pack. "Here," he said, wrapping the hand mirror in a shirt and tucking it in lengthwise. "Keep it safe."

Wordlessly Liza zipped her pack up.

Michael felt like an ass. "Of course." Unable to look at any of them, he hoisted his pack and continued walking along the riverbank.

EIGHTEEN

MAGGIE? WHY THE HELL DID HE CALL ME MAGGIE?

As Liza scrambled over the slippery shoals along the water's edge, she wondered why her pack felt heavier than ever. Was it the snow or the mirror, now bearing the added weight of guilt?

She replayed her argument with Michael as she trudged along, alternately wanting to cry or to tear into him. It wasn't her fault she couldn't come as prepared as an Eagle Scout. Besides, didn't she get some credit for finding the hunting gear and the gun? Like Diego said, that longbow had bought their dinner, and he seemed relieved to have the old gun.

Michael's not being fair, she thought, her stomach tightening. *He has no reason to be so mad.*

She studied Michael's blurred outline as he hiked through the snow in front of her, limping slightly as if he'd wrenched an ankle. He'd changed in the last twenty-four hours. Then again, everything had changed.

The snow added a surreal feeling to the landscape, to her already surreal life. Nothing was as it should be. Not her father, not Uncle Frank, not the place she called home, and not Michael. What was left to hold on to? She had nothing left, just . . . wreckage.

Against the backdrop of falling snow she pictured her father, could see his face clearly, with his arched brow and tousled hair. The thought of him made her fingers dig into her backpack straps.

Anger. That helped.

She wondered how he was negotiating this crisis, the betrayal of his daughter. What a blow to his ego, his only daughter fleeing perfect Novo Mundum for the threats of the outside world. How would he ever put a spin on that? The only good thing about getting caught would be to see her father's humiliation in person.

But as much as she wanted to see her father squirm, she knew she'd come too far: there was no going back. They had to get away. Even if Michael was out of his mind at this moment, she knew he was basically on her side. He wasn't a killer. Her father and uncle, on the other hand . . . She couldn't even begin to fathom what they might be capable of.

She shifted her pack yet again, her breath coming in heavy gasps. The bank had gotten steeper, and her back strained with every new step.

Okay, maybe Michael was right about the mirror. Maybe she shouldn't have brought it. One thing was sure, if she didn't lighten her load, she would end up slowing down the whole group and putting them at risk of capture.

Slowly and carefully, she slipped the pack off her shoulders and swung it in front of her. She had to slide one arm through the loop to hold it up, but she didn't want to stop the group's progress. Checking to make sure no one was looking, she slid the zipper up and reached inside. Her hand closed around the mirror, still draped in her spare T-shirt.

No! she thought angrily. She just couldn't do it. She shouldn't have to. Her mother was the one part of her past she wasn't ashamed of—the only thing she wanted to remember. The mirror would bring her strength, just as Diego said.

But she couldn't keep going with all this weight.

She dug down deeper, finally hitting something large and heavy. At the bottom of her pack, wrapped in black plastic, were the tennis shoes she'd worn through the sewer. She'd kept them, hoping they'd dry out, but they were smelly and half frozen. She'd probably never wear them again.

She reached in the bag with both hands, ripped into the plastic, and yanked out her shoes. Then, before anyone could notice, she tossed them into the woods. The red sneakers bounced off the snow-dusted ground and tumbled before coming to rest on their sides.

There, Liza thought, feeling pleased with herself. Her pack felt much lighter now as she hoisted it back onto her shoulders. Quickening her pace, she took one final glance back at the shoes: wreckage from her old, discarded life.

Good riddance.

NINETEEN

JONAH COULD SEE IT THROUGH THE BINOCULARS, A BRIGHT RED check mark, like a small streak of fresh blood. Was it blood? Was one of his friends injured? The red mark in the snow was definitely something Becker would want to check out.

He glanced up the ridge at the big, muscular brute with a permanent snarl on his face. Just his luck they'd stuck him with the most gung ho Vin Diesel wannabe in the group. Jonah didn't like the way Becker ordered him around, and he hated the way the man spat on the ground each time he brought up the deserters (or "buncha quitters" as he referred to them). Of course, his obsessive zeal to track down Jonah's friends and bring them to justice was probably the reason the captain had paired him with Jonah. Jonah knew this was a test of his loyalty to Novo Mundum. After all, with the exception of Amber, the rest of his friends had gone wrong, taking the boss's daughter with them. Why should anyone at Novo Mundum trust Jonah now?

So Captain Tabori had handpicked him for the search party, and suddenly Jonah had found himself barreling over rocks and debris in a covered jeep, tracking the group with the help of Michael's GPS disk, a very cold, alienating gun in a holster strapped to his thigh.

"Dalton! What's taking you so long?" Becker grumbled.

Jonah gingerly made his way up the hill where Becker stood waiting for him.

"Well?" Becker demanded. "What'd you see?"

Jonah knew he should tell him about the red mark, but he held back. If he could just get Becker to focus on another area, he might be able to sneak away and double back to investigate the red thing. "Nothing," he replied. "In fact, we probably shouldn't head that way. It's the shorter way down, but it looks slippery." At least he wasn't lying. A small tributary dripped down the slope into the river below, covering the side of the hill with patches of ice.

Becker snorted. "What? You afraid of a little ice? Come on. If it's faster, this is the way we're taking."

"No, but Becker, I really think—"

"Quick yapping and fall in line Dal—" Becker suddenly let out a high-pitched yelp and disappeared from sight. A dull crash followed.

Jonah's heart hammered in his chest as he peered over the crest. He couldn't see Becker at all, just a sheer drop to the bottom of the ravine. He cut over to where the slope was manageable and carefully descended. Halfway down he spotted Becker, prone on the ravine, groaning.

"Don't move!" Jonah said.

Becker let out a string of curse words.

Jonah jumped into the ravine. As he approached, he noticed Becker's right leg twisted at an awkward angle.

"Damned if it's not broken," Becker said, beads of sweat on his forehead despite the cold.

"You'd better stay still till I get help. You don't want to injure it more." Jonah pulled a rough wool blanket out of his pack and covered Becker with it. Then he bent down and handed him his canteen. "I'll go get the others."

Becker simply nodded, his face a mixture of pain and humiliation.

"I'll be back soon."

Jonah took off through the trees, heading toward the spot of red. He would fetch help. Just as soon as he investigated that red splotch.

Eventually he found it: a bright red, discarded tennis shoe. Its mate lay a couple of feet away. Jonah picked it up and studied it. He recognized them—Liza's shoes. He'd seen her wearing them tons of times. And judging by the light snow cover, the shoes had been tossed fairly recently. Maybe a half hour, tops.

He buried the shoes in the snow to prevent anyone else spying them, then took off through the trees.

There they were. Less than a football field away. He felt a pang of pity seeing them trudge forward in a crooked line, their bodies bent against the cold. But except for Michael's obvious limp they all appeared to be okay.

Now that he'd caught up with them, Jonah wasn't sure how to proceed. He'd decided that the thing to do was talk some sense into them, make them change their minds about leaving Novo Mundum behind. But now, with his friends a stone's throw away, he wasn't sure how to accomplish that.

He slipped back into the forest and ran downhill until he was almost even with them. Then he slowly strode toward the riverbank, his heartbeat echoing in his ears.

Suddenly Diego barked out an order and everyone else ducked behind the embankment. The next thing he knew an arrow went whizzing past him, shooting into a tree trunk with a sickening *thwack!*

Jonah slunk behind a large spruce, breathing heavily and holding his left ear. He was bleeding. The arrow must have grazed him. Jonah swallowed hard. He'd forgotten what a great shot Diego was.

Slowly and shakily, he pulled the gun from its holster and slid sideways around the tree. The gun felt heavy in his hand. He'd always hated guns, hated what they did to people. Back in Atlanta, before Strain 7, his cousin Derek had found out how easy it was for things to go wrong with a gun. A liquor store robbery went bad, the owner had been shot, and Derek had gone to prison, died there when Strain 7 hit.

"Jonah?" he heard Irene call, followed by murmurs and shushing sounds.

"It's me," he cried. "I—I just want to talk!"

"If you just want to talk, why are you pointing a gun at us?" Diego shouted.

"You shot me," Jonah answered. "I'm bleeding."

"You'll survive if you drop the gun." Diego's fingers curled tightly around the bowstring. A fresh arrow had been cocked, its titanium tip directed right at Jonah's chest.

"I'm by myself, I promise." Jonah took a deep breath and dropped the gun to his side. "Don't shoot me and I won't shoot you," he said.

"Whatever you have to say, say it quick," Diego muttered.

"Guys, you have to stop. You have to come back."

Liza stepped forward. "Did my father send you? How many people are looking for us?"

Jonah's mind wheeled for a moment. "About thirty," he lied. "They're combing the entire forest and it's only a matter of time before they find you."

"Thirty?" Diego scoffed. "You don't have twenty to spare. We'll take our chances."

"You don't understand!" Jonah pleaded. "They . . . We . . . We're supposed to shoot you if you don't come."

Diego's mouth curled sardonically. "I'm not surprised."

"But if you come with me now, no one will get hurt," Jonah continued. "We can work this all out."

"You're living in a fantasyland," Diego snapped. "If we go back, they'll kill us."

"That's not true!"

"They almost killed me, and that was before I struck out against them," Diego said. "I'd rather risk my life out here in a blizzard than back at Novo Mundum."

Jonah turned to Michael. "Michael, listen to reason! This is suicide! You're better off in Novo Mundum."

Michael lowered his head, weary, defeated. "Yeah, right," Michael scoffed. "We'll head back and join Finch and Gabe. That place killed them, Jonah. I'm done with it."

Jonah turned toward Keely and Irene.

"What about you two? You were both chosen. You know they won't do anything to hurt you."

Irene shook her head indignantly. "Jonah, they were dragging me off to quarantine like I was infected with a fatal virus. They were going to eliminate all of us."

Jonah let out a breath, frustrated with all of them. They were making such a huge mistake, making things impossible for him. How could he get through to them?

"Time's up," Diego said, pulling back the bowstring. "Now holster the gun and get on your way."

Jonah balked. He couldn't give up, couldn't let Irene die out here.

"Put the gun away," Diego said more firmly.

He stared at the gun quivering in his hand. He

wanted to put it away, but the hand wouldn't obey.

"Do you really think you could shoot us?" Diego asked, taunting. "Do you think you have the nerve? Think you have the skill to squeeze off a shot before I release this arrow into your gut?"

"Diego," Irene gasped. "You wouldn't."

"Go ahead." Diego continued to stare Jonah down. "Give me a reason."

Irene turned toward Jonah and pressed her gloved hands together, pleading. "Just put down the gun. Let us go, Jonah. I know you want to believe in Novo Mundum, but we won't be safe there. Liza might be spared, but they'll kill the rest of us."

Jonah thought about the security briefing before the search party had been released and Frank's shoot-to-kill command for everyone except Liza. He knew Irene was right. Frank and Captain Tabori considered his friends too much of a liability to be allowed to live.

Diego's voice suddenly cut through his thoughts. "I'm going to count to ten," he called. "Then I let the arrow fly. It's your call." He readied his bow. "Ten . . . nine . . ."

"Diego!" Irene screamed.

"Eight . . . seven . . ."

"You've got to promise me . . ." Jonah began.

"Six . . ."

"Promise you won't let any harm come to Novo Mundum!"

"Five . . ."

"I promise!" Irene said. "*We* promise!"

He peered into her eyes, weighing her words.

"Four . . . three. . . two . . ."

"Okay." Jonah holstered the gun and Diego lifted his chin, though the arrow stayed poised and ready to fire.

"Thank you." Irene's voice trembled with relief.

Jonah stared at her tear-streaked face, wanting to hold her, to reassure her that everything would be fine, though he knew it would be a lie. Irene wouldn't make it at Novo Mundum anymore. She'd been given a chance there, but she'd rejected what they had to offer.

They all had.

And now he was stuck trying to do the right thing, whatever that was. He looked down at the ground and wished he'd never caught up with them. "Just go," he said quietly. "Go, and I'll throw them off your trail."

He could hear them shuffling past, resuming their path beside the swirling stream. By the time he looked up, they were several yards away.

Jonah watched until Irene's dark jacket faded into the thickening snowfall. Then he headed up the ridge to double back and find help for Becker.

TWENTY

WE ARE GOING TO DIE.

The realization settled upon Liza with all the numbing power of the gathering snow. It wasn't as frightening as she had expected death to be; in fact, the prospect of eternal sleep in the snow seemed preferable to the blistering wind and ice on her face. She recalled past news reports—back when there was actual news—of people getting caught in sudden blizzards, wandering about lost and confused, until they ultimately dropped dead from exposure.

Would that be their fate? It just wouldn't be fair to have come this far only to succumb to the elements.

Most of all, Liza hated the idea of losing to her father. She couldn't let him win. And so she hobbled along the icy rocks behind Michael's blurry outline, trusting that the others were still in front of him.

Just then Michael turned and reached out for her, shouting something in the screaming wind. Diego was coming down the line, pushing them ahead, yelling something she couldn't hear. Blindly Liza followed him up toward the tree line. There, nestled between two large spruce trees, was a ramshackle hunter's cabin—a crooked structure fashioned out of logs and crusty with mud.

Finally, a break.

Liza braced herself as Diego pushed open the heavy oak door. She prayed that she wouldn't see any bodies, rotting corpses from Strain 7, or signs of bloodshed from the violence that had ensued. She'd read enough news accounts early on to know what he was checking for, and she'd seen the handful of dead bodies they had encountered in other houses they'd passed. Everyone here thought she was some bubble girl, a tender little lotus blossom, but they were wrong. They didn't know her, and, except for Michael, they didn't really try to change that.

Peering in behind Diego, she caught sight of a dim, dusty interior. The windows were caked with snow and dark gray light seeped in, barely illuminating the packed-dirt floor and a splintery, hand-hewn bench.

"It's good," Diego pronounced.

Relieved, Liza stepped inside, the sudden absence of wind and swirling snow creating an eerie void.

"Thank God," she said quietly, collapsing on the bench. She looked up at Michael, but nothing registered on his face as he limped past her into the dark shadows of the cabin.

A sudden movement to her left startled her and Liza turned to see a large, brown rat staring at her. She let out a small squeal and the rat scurried into a crack in the log wall.

"Good. Stay away," she said.

"I kind of hope he comes back," Diego said, studying the crack. "Sometimes there's good meat on those." He turned toward Michael. "Michael, can you give me a hand? I need your help cutting some firewood."

No answer. Liza shot a look at Michael, who staggered slowly toward the back of the cabin. "Sorry, Diego, I . . . *aaaugh.*" With a groan, Michael slid down against the wall, one leg sliding out from under him.

"What's wrong?" Diego asked.

"My foot." Michael nodded down at his left leg before tilting back his head and shutting his eyes against the pain.

"Let me see." Irene bent down, undid his boot, and carefully pulled it off.

Keely shone the flashlight on his foot, where the skin was a sickly waxy color.

"It's frostbite," Irene said, her voice filled with dread. She picked up the boot and examined it. "Michael, why didn't you tell us your shoe was ripped?"

Liza felt a small spark of vindication. *Looks like Mr. Judgmental didn't come so prepared himself,* she thought, remembering the way he'd blown up at her over her lack of warm clothes.

Still, almost immediately she felt terrible for having the thought and realized how worried she was for him. His toes were bluish white. She took a seat next to Michael and reached for his hand as Irene recalled the treatment for frostbite.

Liza glanced at each person's chapped face, reading Michael's pain, Keely's half-masked concerns, and the grief behind Irene's eyes. Only Diego seemed completely at ease—strong and energized and undaunted by the blizzard. The others were stretched to their limits, but Diego, he was in his element.

"Is he going to be okay?" Liza whispered to Irene.

"I think so," Irene answered as she removed Michael's other boot and socks. "We need that fire, though."

Liza rose to her feet. "I'll help you with firewood, Diego."

He studied her for a moment. "Okay. You collect as much moss and lichen as you can while I cut down some twigs. It'll be hard to find anything dry, but—"

"No problem."

"Good." Diego nodded, almost approving.

As she followed him back out into the storm, Liza sensed that they were starting to accept her. Finally.

TWENTY-ONE

IRENE POKED AT THE SMALL FIRE WITH A PIECE OF KINDLING, watching the tiny shower of sparks shoot up from the smoldering fragments of wood. Then she tossed the stick into the flames and sat back against the cabin's bumpy wall, draping her blanket over her shoulders.

It was unnaturally quiet. After countless hours the wind had finally died down outside. Diego had left soon after with his bow, hoping to find food, and everyone else was stretched out on bedrolls, deep in sleep.

Irene had offered to keep watch. As it was, she was too wound up to sleep and wanted to keep a close eye on Michael's foot. Frostbite. Probably painful. It seemed to be thawing out, but it was still too soon to tell whether or not he'd be able to walk on it. She looked at him now, his jaw muscles flexing as he slept fitfully. What would they do if he couldn't continue? Diego had muttered something about building a sled to drag him on, but that was impractical, and she knew Michael would never go for it.

Her eyes traveled over to Liza, who lay sprawled next to Michael, one hand resting on his chest. She looked so young, with her mouth open slightly and her face smoothed of worry lines. Irene was surprised at how well Liza was handling this whole ordeal. She'd gone through so much in the past few days, her world shifting in devastating ways.

Irene wondered about her own father and brother. Where were they? Did they know she was gone yet? How would they take it? Would they blame her? A week before she'd left, they had been making plans for Thanksgiving, talking about ways to re-create the traditions they'd shared in Philadelphia when her mother was alive. Now Irene wondered if they would celebrate without her. . . .

Keely sat up in her sleeping bag and rolled over to face the fire. Irene was surprised to see she was wide awake.

"Are you thirsty?" Irene asked.

"I'm fine. Can't sleep, though. If you want to lie down, I'll keep watch for a while."

"No. I wouldn't be able to sleep either." Irene picked up another stick and began poking the fire again, hypnotizing herself with the tiny sprays of embers.

"You miss your dad and brother, don't you?"

Irene stabbed at the fire. Was she that obvious? "Yeah," she admitted. "I was just thinking about them."

Keely laid her head on her open palm. "I'm sorry you had to leave them behind."

"I feel guilty. Like I should have explained all this to them. When I think of the future, of trying to reconnect with them, it's overwhelming. All the craziness in the Big Empty and the rules in the Occupied Zone . . . What are the chances of finding them?"

Keely shook her head, her hair golden in the firelight. "I try not to think of the future. It's all out of control. Sometimes I marvel that any of us even survived Strain 7, let alone the zoo of a government that sliced up the states. Or this blizzard."

Survival. It had been relatively easy for Irene with her father taking care of her. How had Diego managed all those months, alone on that small farm? And in the end it wasn't the isolation that had stopped him, but a soldier's bullet.

As the fire crackled, Irene flashed back to the standoff with Jonah earlier that day. Diego facing a gun again and not even flinching. In fact, he'd seemed ready to fire off another arrow at Jonah, eager for an excuse for violence. "I guess you could say that about all of us. We're survivors. Even Jonah."

"Jonah . . ." Keely flopped onto her bedroll. "I can't believe he pointed a gun at us."

"What about Diego? He was so intense with the longbow. Jonah never would have actually shot any of us. Diego should have known that."

"I wouldn't bet on it," Keely said. "That's the thing about a cult mentality. Jonah's not thinking for himself. He's letting Dr. Slattery do it for him. And if Slattery said shoot . . ."

"He did let us go. He still has control of his own decisions." Irene hugged her knees to her chest. "It's Diego I'm worried about. He's just looking for a chance to hurt someone. He never puts down the bow, did you notice that?"

"Think about what he's been through," Keely said. "He's probably just wants to make double sure no one ever gets the jump on him again."

"I hope you're right," Irene said, though deep down, she wasn't convinced. She could understand it if Diego were acting out of fear or self-defense. But watching him square off with Jonah, his hands steady and his eyes cold as steel, she'd realized he was tapping into a much darker place.

And that scared her.

TWENTY-TWO

IF ONLY THEY'D SENT ME BACK WITH BECKER.

As Jonah crept up the snow-covered slope behind Captain Tabori and the guard who went by the name "River," he wondered if they would ever make it back to Paradise City. Although the search party was down to three now, Captain Tabori seemed more determined than ever to stay on task, to find Liza.

"I'm not going back without her," the woman had shouted through her scarf, making Jonah secretly cop to his biggest mistake.

He hadn't even tried to convince Liza to come back without the others.

How stupid. Of course, the team needed to bring her

back. She was the prize, her father's pride and joy. God, he was stupid.

The captain motioned Jonah to move faster up the hill, where another hunting shack sat under drifts of snow. Another place to check, another venue for Captain Tabori to use her detective skills in tracking his friends. This really sucked.

Jonah stationed himself near the door, but the captain held up her hand, gesturing for them to wait, her head cocked as she listened for noise. She checked Jonah and River, then held up three fingers. Two . . . one . . .

River jumped forward and kicked the door, which instantly collapsed inward in a cloud of snow and splinters. Then he and Jonah rushed into the cabin, followed closely by Captain Tabori.

But the place was empty except for a scattering of leaves across the dirt floor.

"Damn!" Tabori kicked up a spray of pine needles.

Jonah shared her frustration, mostly because he wanted to get back. For the captain their entire mission had been one embarrassment after another. First they couldn't find the trail, then Becker got hurt and one volunteer had to pull him back to the jeep. They were down to a team of three and had run over her "twenty-four hours, tops" prediction.

Tabori shouldered her rifle, stooped over, and pushed away the layer of sticks and nettles. Underneath lay a clump of gray ashes still steaming slightly in the freezing air. "A fire pit," she exclaimed. "They were just here."

Jonah studied the evidence with some relief. The entire time the search party rode out the blizzard in their makeshift camp, he had worried about his friends. At least they'd survived.

"All right." Captain Tabori shook the snow out of her scarf as she paced the cabin. "We're going to concentrate on the riverbed. It would take them right to the city and it would hide their tracks better. But luckily for us, it also doesn't provide much cover. If we hustle, we should be able to spot them at the next ridge. Come on. Move!"

Jonah balked, all jammed up. After the face-off with his friends, he knew they would never give up. Hell, Diego would sooner get shot than come back with them. Of course, he'd also take at least one of them down with an arrow first.

This was not going to be a happy reunion.

As they hiked along the frozen bank, Captain Tabori pointed out the footprints in the snow. "There's no snow on top of them, which means the tracks were made after the flurries stopped early this morning," she said. "My guess is they're not too far ahead of us."

Jonah couldn't help but notice the eager tone in her voice and the slight bounce in her stride. She wanted the mission over, one way or another. And he had an uneasy feeling she wouldn't hesitate to end it with her AK-47.

With some dread, Jonah plodded along behind her, arms out to maintain his balance over the icy riverbank, his mind distracted with thoughts of his friends.

If only he could warn them.

Just then his foot landed on an unsteady stone and he lurched forward and slid to the ground, the fall pressing the gun into his hip. He stood, dusted off the snow, and slid the gun out of its holster as an idea germinated.

A warning shot. If Irene and the others were as close as the captain predicted, they'd hear it for sure.

He pushed on, breathing deeply to steady his nerves. He had to do this just right, didn't want to be too obvious.

He saw his chance when they reached an uneven patch of ice-frosted gravel. Very slippery. Treacherous. Perfect.

Carefully he pointed the barrel skyward, closed his eyes, and squeezed the trigger.

109

The noise was deafening—an explosion of sound that swelled outward, clattering off the surrounding hills.

Captain Tabori whirled around, fixing him with a death glare.

"Sorry," he said, wincing against the blast. "I slipped and it just went off."

Tabori frowned. "All right, men. Double your pace," she ordered. "Thanks to you, Dalton, we no longer have the element of surprise."

TWENTY-THREE

DIEGO'S PULSE QUICKENED AT THE LOUD REPORT. HE KNEW exactly what it was.

"What the hell was that?" Keely asked, turning in a slow circle and staring into the surrounding trees.

"A gunshot," Diego answered. "Not even a mile away. Sounds like they've picked up our trail."

"What if it's not the search party?" Michael said. "What if it's someone else?"

"Like who?" Keely asked. "The Slash?"

"Either way, we aren't sticking around to find out," Diego muttered. "We've got to keep moving and we've got to conceal ourselves."

"But where?" Irene gestured around them. The forest on their side of the river had thinned considerably.

They were now heading into ranch land full of rotting stables, barbed-wire fences, and flat fields of snow. No place to take cover. They were sitting ducks.

Unless . . .

Diego wandered along the bank, gauging the expanse of frozen river in front of him. "We can cross," he said, pointing to the heavily wooded hills on the opposite side. "Right here."

He scanned a path where the river was only about sixty feet across and covered with white ice.

"Are you crazy?" Keely exclaimed. "I grew up in L.A., but even I know that you don't cross ice that covers running water. It's probably not frozen solid."

"We'll cross on our stomachs to spread our weight more evenly," Diego said. "Just inch yourself along. If we hurry, we'll make it to the other side before anyone catches up with us."

Irene grabbed his arm. "But Diego, we don't know if the ice will hold. The river hasn't been frozen long."

"It's our best chance. I'll go first so if the ice breaks, I'll be the one who falls through."

"No," Michael said suddenly. "I'll go first. We need you more."

Diego shook his head. "Come on, Michael—"

"We don't have time to argue!" Michael interrupted.

Before Diego could stop him, Michael was stretched out on the ice in front of them, crawling across the river.

"You guys go next," Diego said. "If it holds Michael, it'll hold each of you. I'll bring up the rear." That way he could look out for the search party.

"Okay," Liza said solemnly. She flopped down on the ice behind Michael and edged along after him.

"That's right," Diego instructed as Keely followed Liza. "Nice and easy. Distribute your weight as evenly as possible."

Irene stepped to the frozen riverbank and glanced back at Diego, her breath a puff of white.

"It's okay," he said. "I'll be right behind you."

"I know. Just . . . be careful." She was giving him that look again, studying him warily as if he were a pet project for med school. Which totally bugged him. Irene was great when she wasn't smothering him with *ER* crap.

Once she got moving, Diego slipped his bow and arrow into his pack and squatted down. Up ahead, Michael was halfway across. Behind them, no signs of anyone approaching yet. Maybe, just maybe, their luck would hold out for a while.

Diego stretched out on the ice and started dragging himself along, keeping his eye on the undersides of Irene's boots as they scooted along in front of him. The cold penetrated his layers of clothing and his gunshot wound throbbed in protest, but he forced himself to keep moving.

He scraped his right elbow forward, cognizant of a cracking noise below. No, it wasn't frozen solid. Maybe just a few inches of ice. Maybe less. But he couldn't think about that now. He had to trust that his friends were getting across. If he lifted his chin, he could make out Michael already standing on land, but he didn't

want to waste a movement, didn't want to apply unnecessary pressure on the ice.

Just a little while longer, he prayed silently. *We're
almost there.*

Ahead of him, Irene scrabbled up, wiping snow from
her pants. Snow-covered evergreens hugged the steep
hillside in front of her. Branches woven so tightly
together, anything could hide behind them. A perfect
getaway spot.

"We did it." Irene bent down and held out her hand.

"I'm fine." Diego rolled off the ice and stood up to
survey the others, their cheeks rosy with a sense of
accomplishment. Good. They needed the boost. "Let's
keep moving," he said, shaking the numbness out of his
limbs. "This isn't over yet."

TWENTY-FOUR

IRENE LAY BACK AGAINST THE TRUNK OF A BARE, SKELETAL-looking tree, finally allowing herself a rest. This latest hike had been the most difficult so far. Since they'd crossed the river, the landscape had gradually become more rough-hewn and perilous—steep, ice-covered hills with craggy, colorful clefts in their sides. They'd spotted a couple of towns in the distance, each one beckoning to them like an oasis in the desert, but Diego had steered them away, saying they were too visible, too easily accessible. Instead he led them deep into the forest, always aiming for the darkest, thickest clusters of trees. Occasionally Irene would see Keely checking her compass to make sure they were still headed northeast, and they always were. Somehow Diego always knew.

The last couple of hours had been one long exhausting climb. When they finally reached the top of the ridge, Diego found a spot under some tall pines where they could rest while he looked for food. They decided against a fire since the smoke might alert the search party, but Irene felt comfortable inside her parka from exertion and was relieved to stop for a short rest and a drink of water.

"I wonder how far we are from the train yards," Keely said as she dropped her mittens to the ground and unscrewed her canteen.

"I haven't even seen railroad tracks," Irene said.

"That'll be a score," Michael said, shifting his feet gingerly. "Climbing onto a train, out of the snow and rain. I plan to sleep for a week, maybe two."

Irene nodded, happy to see shades of the old Michael. The rough mending they'd done on his boot with dried rabbit skin seemed to be working out, and his toes seemed to be holding up.

When Keely passed her the canteen, Irene noticed her right hand shaking. For some reason, it hurt like hell. She took a drink, then handed the canteen back and pressed her left thumb into the pain's epicenter. She continued massaging while Keely searched her pack for vegetable jerky and Michael and Liza shared a drink.

Irene moved up the hill, wondering what she'd done to her hand. The only thing she could figure was that she'd probably wrenched it pulling herself over an icy boulder. She found a sheltered spot under a tree, where she leaned back and closed her eyes.

"Did you hurt yourself?" Diego crouched beside her, spiking his longbow into the snow.

"Not really," she said. "It's probably just a sprain."

"Here. Let me." He pressed her slender hand between his palms and massaged.

Irene could feel her cheeks grow warm. They hadn't been this close since the night they'd spent in the shed, hadn't really touched each other in the chaos of fleeing through the snowy countryside.

Diego watched her intently, then leaned closer. She could see the light playing off his hair, noticed the dark stubble on his jawline, and then he was right before her, becoming her entire view. He cupped her face. "I miss you," he murmured.

"Me too."

He leaned down, closing the final inches between them, and pressed his lips to hers. Breathless, Irene wrapped her arms around him and held on tight.

The kiss deepened as they both explored inside each other's coats. Diego pulled Irene's hood over her head and pressed her down into the frozen ground. Looking up at the waving treetops while Diego's lips nuzzled her ear, her neck, her collarbone, Irene marveled at how surprising this world was. One day you faced death, the next you were kissing in a winter wonderland.

As he shifted his body over hers, she pressed her lips up to touch his. She wanted this—*needed* this. She couldn't stop herself if she tried.

They rolled sideways, clutching tightly to each

other, and suddenly Diego tensed. He jerked backward and let out a small cry of pain.

"Your leg!" She sat up quickly, kicking herself. "Are you okay?"

"I'm fine," he said breathlessly, clutching his left thigh.

"You should let me take a look."

"No. It's all right."

"Please, Diego. It will only take a second."

"I'm *fine.*" He scrambled to his feet, turned away.

"Stop being stubborn," she said in a low, measured voice. "We all need you. And if you don't take care of yourself, you—"

"*Shhh!*" Diego held up a hand and stalked to the brink of the outcropping.

"I won't *shhh!*" she said, trotting after him. "This is important. We need—"

In a sudden movement Diego spun toward her, grabbed her shoulders, and clamped a hand over her mouth. Irene froze, her heart racing.

"Be quiet," he murmured into her ear. "I think I hear something."

She stared at him. The anger was gone from his face, replaced by a wary alertness. Irene nodded solemnly and he released his grip.

Slowly and silently, Diego crouched down and crawled out of the trees and to a vantage point overlooking the valley. Irene followed, trying not to make noise.

Sure enough, they could see the search party down

below—three people weaving through the trees near the base of the cliff overlooking the river, Jonah straggling at the end.

"Damn it," Diego muttered, his jaw flexing rhythmically.

"What do we do?" Irene asked in a faint whisper.

She waited for Diego to begin barking out orders, spurring her and the others on to safety. Instead he stared down the mountain as if trying to gauge something. He seemed to be measuring, then sat back with resolution. "Come on," he muttered. Together they scrambled and rolled downhill in the snow to the tree-shaded outcropping where the others were waiting.

Diego hobbled right up to Michael. "Give me the gun," he demanded.

An icy sensation skittered down Irene's spine. *What does he want that for?*

Michael appeared to have similar reservations. "Why?"

"Just give it to me. *Now!*" Diego urged. "I don't have time to explain!"

Michael studied Diego, hesitating. Finally he unsheathed the gun and handed it over. The girls exchanged fearful glances.

"No, Diego. Don't," Irene said as he started back up the cliff. "Wait!" She reached out and grabbed his arm.

He whirled around, staring at her hand on his arm. "You don't trust me, do you?" he asked, his expression darkening.

"Of course I do," she said, but it didn't even sound convincing to her. Her voice was high and weak and seemed to fly away on the wind. "But . . ."

"Leave me alone." He wrenched his arm away and charged up the cliff, his left leg dragging slightly behind him.

Irene followed him, Keely beside her, but Diego was a few steps ahead, already positioning himself at the edge of the precipice.

"Oh God," Keely gasped as he raised his arm to fire.

Only then did Irene realize he was aiming out instead of down.

The gun went off with a loud crack, the shot echoing in the distance. Soon after there came a loud rumbling sound. The ground beneath Irene's boots vibrated slightly, and she glanced out through the trees in time to see a blinding rush of white go hurtling down the mountainside, along with several large rocks and boulders.

An avalanche!

After a long moment the rattling stopped. Irene clambered to the brink and looked down. A mountain of snow, ice, and a few crushed trees now lay between them and the search party. In the clouds of powder she could just make out the three figures on the other side of the debris—still alive, still moving.

Slowly and stiffly, Diego trudged back down, passing her without meeting her eyes. She could almost hear what he was thinking—that she should have trusted him.

Should have. But didn't.

TWENTY-FIVE

A LOUD KNOCK SOUNDED ON THE DOOR, WAKING AMBER FROM deep sleep. She rubbed her eyes and lifted herself onto her elbows. "Come in."

A round, middle-aged woman entered. Oh yeah—her. She had come a couple of times before, but Amber couldn't remember her name. *Haddie? Patty? Chatty?*

"Good morning!" the woman sang out, setting a plate of food on the tray next to the bed.

"Morning," Amber mumbled. *Caddie? Batty? Bratty?*

"I brought good stuff," the woman warbled. "They're saving up the meats for our upcoming Thanksgiving feast, so today . . ." She removed the cloth that covered the meal. "Vegetable medley!"

Maddie! Amber thought. How could she forget? The woman's voice always drove her *mad.*

"Oh, yum," Amber replied, staring at the gloop on the thick plastic platter. She knew the food prep people were trying to use up some of the vegetables they didn't get around to preserving for winter, but they still hadn't figured out the whole taste factor.

"So." Maddie smiled at her expectantly. "How are you feeling?"

"Like a beached whale."

"Oh, you," the woman said, waving her hand as if to brush away her response.

Hey, you asked, Amber thought irritably.

As she sat up in bed, Maddie hastily propping her backside with pillows, Amber reminded herself to be nice. After all, these people didn't have to bring her food and check on her throughout the day. They did it out of the goodness of their hearts so that she didn't have to waddle her fat ass down to the food lines and risk not only fainting spells and blood clots, but the wrath of Dr. MacTavish as well.

Of course, there was another reason why they volunteered. . . .

"So . . . there's still no word from the search party," Maddie said, settling herself onto Keely's bed. "I mean, not since they brought back that one man with the broken leg."

"Mmm?" Amber replied, taking a big bite of food—if only to avoid having to talk.

The woman was trying her best to sound matter-of-fact,

but it was pointless. All of the volunteers wanted the same thing—inside information on Amber's runaway roommate and friends. It blew their blissed-out minds that anyone would actually want to leave Novo Mundum. Especially when two of those people were Michael the Boy Wonder and Dr. Slattery's daughter.

They'd even begun circulating their own bizarre theories: that Michael had gone crazy, killed Gabe, then kidnapped Liza and the others at gunpoint. Or that Michael and Keely had contracted a horrible virus on their mission that drove them crazy, and it spread to Irene, Liza, and Diego before Dr. Slattery discovered it and they took off to avoid being put in quarantine.

If it wasn't so pathetic, it would be funny.

"It's just so strange, don't you think?" Maddie leaned forward, elbows on her knees, propping her chubby face with her hand. "Was your roommate acting weird? Did you have any idea at all she would do something like this?"

Amber tapped a finger against her chin and glanced up at the ceiling, pretending to ponder the question. She had to be careful. "No. Absolutely no clue," she replied. "But who cares? Good riddance. It's not like I miss having to share this place with someone. Especially someone I can't trust."

Even as she spoke, Amber felt a wistful tug somewhere around her bulging belly. She really did miss Keely. A lot. All her life she'd been used to having her own space, and rooming with Keely had cramped her style a bit. But still, she even missed the things that drove her crazy, like

Keely's habit of flinging open the curtains in the morning, even when Amber wanted to sleep in, or those damn hospital corners that left the sheets too tight after she made the beds. Now Keely's bed lay neat and empty and Amber rarely left hers.

Maddie made sympathetic clicking sounds with her tongue and Amber decided to take it even further. The more she could come off as a victim in this whole crazy mess, the better.

"But to tell you the truth, I just really feel betrayed, you know?" she added, staring glumly into her lap. "I mean, I thought she was my friend. I thought she'd be here to help me when the baby came. But now she's going to miss everything."

Amber paused. She hadn't taken any more bites of food, but a bristly lump suddenly wedged in her throat, making her eyes mist up and her nostrils grow moist and tingly. She realized she really was hurt by their leaving. She knew beyond any doubt that they'd done the right thing, and she was also absolutely positive she'd made the right choice by staying behind. But she couldn't help feeling abandoned.

At least they still had each other. Who did she have? Grumpy Dr. MacTavish? Jonah—who was out there this very minute hunting down his former friends? Just thinking about him made her want to puke.

Amber gave a loud sniff and a tear skittered down her cheek and plopped onto her tray. *Damn hormones!* she thought, wiping her face with her sleeve. *Turning me into a wuss!*

"Don't worry, dear," Maddie said, patting Amber's hand. "We're here to help. You won't go through this alone."

Amber studied the big, kind, naïve woman. "Thanks," she mumbled. She wanted to give in to the compassion, to tell herself everything would be fine for her and the baby. But she'd been disappointed way too many times to let that happen.

Nothing had changed. She might be surrounded by smiling, caring faces, but she was still totally alone. And the overriding rule was the same:

Trust no one.

TWENTY-SIX

KEELY WAS COLD AND TIRED. COLD EVEN THOUGH THE SNOWFALL
had eased somewhat, and so tired of walking. She figured that the hiking of the past few days had given her
enough aerobic training to last the next year. But
mainly she was tired of the continuous bickering among
the two couples she found herself hiking with—the
frostiness between them was almost worse than the
wintry winds.

It had been two days since the avalanche that had
cut them off from the search party, and no one would
say aloud what each was surely thinking: that they'd
gotten away. Hope was such a brittle thing in their situ-
ation, it was better not to take it out and polish it.

"No, we can't take a break now," Diego argued, shaking

wet snow from his dark hair. "It's too late. We need to press on until we find a place to camp for the night."

"But Michael has been on his foot way too long," Irene countered. "And I can tell you're in pain. You're trying to hide it, but it shows."

"News flash. Sleeping on icicles won't make us better either," Diego snapped.

Irene let out a sigh. "I'm not saying we should stop for the night. I'm saying that you need—"

"You don't know what I need!" Diego seethed. "*I* know what I need. At least trust me on that."

Everyone fell quiet, and Keely politely averted her gaze from Irene and Diego, staring instead at the darkening sky. The clouds were gray and ominous, like gigantic piles of steel wool. She agreed with Diego that they should keep going until they found a safe camping spot. But she wasn't going to voice that unless absolutely necessary. Besides, she also agreed with Irene. Diego was obviously hurting and was just too pigheaded to admit it.

As they trudged along in weighty silence, the path suddenly dipped and curved. Keely jogged down the icy slope, the impact of each step throbbing in her overwrought joints.

"Look!" Liza cried as they stepped out of a thicket of trees. The land bent sharply left, leading into a frozen lagoon. Trapped in the ice were a couple of paddleboats, their color stripped down by the elements to faint yellow and blue streaks. A broken canoe lay on the small beach next to the remains of a rusted swing set. And up the hill just beyond the playground lay a sludge-filled swimming pool and a scattering of overturned patio furniture.

"It's an old resort," Keely remarked.

"I don't like this," Diego muttered. "Let's stay back in the trees just in case."

They stealthily crept through the forest, skirting the recreational area until they came to a parking lot. A wooden sign stood under a tangle of fallen limbs.

"Di-something," Keely read, squinting at the carved script letters. "Di . . . Point?"

Liza gasped. "Diamond Point? I know this place. I thought it looked familiar. My parents used to bring me here when I was little." She pointed to a tree-covered knoll just beyond the parking lot. "The main buildings are on the other side of that hill."

"This would be a good spot to camp, don't you think?" Irene asked Diego, rather tentatively.

He shook his head. "It's too good. There could be other people here. Soldiers, maybe."

"Or it could be empty. And there could be supplies in there. Food. Dry clothes," Keely said, feeling hopeful.

Liza turned to Michael. "What do you think? Should we go in?"

"Whatever," he said, stone-faced. "Don't ask me."

"You don't have to be rude," Liza responded, emotion shattering her voice. "I'm only asking your opinion!"

Not again. The stress was almost palpable. Keely

could feel it gathering around their group like storm clouds. She couldn't take much more.

"I'll go check it out," Keely offered.

Everyone turned to stare at her.

"No," Diego said. "No way are you going in there alone."

"She won't be." Michael stepped forward. "I'll go in with her."

Keely could see Liza's back stiffen, her eyes narrowing, though she didn't object.

Diego surveyed Keely and Michael. "Okay," he said. "Be extra quiet and check the place thoroughly for people. Don't waste time looking for supplies yet. We'll cover you from here."

"Got it," Keely said. Michael nodded.

They shed their packs, Michael carrying only his gun and Keely holding the flashlight. Together they circled the parking lot under the cover of the trees. Sure enough, two buildings lay at the bottom of the hill. Keely scanned the surrounding snow for fresh footprints or wheel tracks, but there was nothing. And a good deal of snow was piled up in front of the doorways. It certainly looked abandoned. They crept toward the first building, a long, narrow log cabin. Keely wiped the frost off the lower-left corner of a window and peered through the glass. Inside, she could see an Olympic-size swimming pool that was empty except for a shallow layer of trash.

Michael jerked his head sideways to indicate that they should move on to the next building. He crouched down and trotted to the nearest corner, Keely following right behind him. The other structure was another log cabin but much larger. It was two stories high, with several redwood balconies built along the western side.

Keely peered through a nearby window but could only make out darkness inside.

"Let's try the door," Michael whispered.

Again as they tramped toward the front entrance, Keely noted the buildup of snow—over two feet, with no signs of any recent disturbance. If someone was inside, they hadn't left the place for a few days.

Michael held his gun high and went in first. After a few seconds he motioned for Keely to follow.

They picked their way through a large, dim reception/dining area, stepping over piles of broken dishes, ripped linens, and broken furniture. They searched both floors—no signs of people at all. Walking back down the stairs, they finally allowed themselves to talk.

"Well, someone was here at one point, and they really trashed the place," Keely observed, sidestepping an upturned piano. "You think soldiers did this?"

Michael shook his head. "I doubt it. Look at that." He pointed at one wall.

Keely aimed the flashlight beam onto the wood paneling. A row of paintings hung crookedly, all western-themed portraits of pioneers and cowboys. Someone had sliced open the canvas on each subject's right cheek.

"The Slash." Keely winced. "Think they could still be around?"

"Nah. Looks like they grabbed whatever they wanted and took off."

"But they left some treasure behind," Keely said, shining the flashlight over the heaps of junk on the floor. "Blankets, maybe a can of food somewhere." She kicked an amber-colored glass bottle that rolled into an empty, square-shaped liquor jug.

"I'd say liquor was their priority," Michael said, leaning down behind the bar, lifting up discarded empty bottles. "Anything they could scrounge out of the bar." He bent down and pulled out a green bottle. "This one's still full."

"Champagne!" Keely exclaimed, glancing at the label.

A grin buoyed Michael's worn-down features. "Let's open it." He braced the bottle against his thighs and fumbled with the plastic cork.

"Shouldn't we wait and share with the others?" Keely asked.

Michael shook his head. "We'll save some for them. Right now my foot's killing me. Let's just rest here for a minute and have a drink. Then we'll go get them."

"Okay."

The bottle uncorked with a sudden *pop* and foamy liquid streamed down the sides. Keely managed to find two relatively clean-looking glasses among the rubble and the two of them sat down with their backs against the cabinet, sipping champagne.

It fizzed through Keely, soothing her tired, chilled body and dulling her senses. After days of being in high-stress mode, she welcomed the relief.

She took a big gulp, leaned her head back, and closed her eyes. An odd sense of déjà vu came over her. Scrounging a drink in a St. Louis mall. The Diet Coke that Gabe had scavenged when they were holed up in the mall during their mission. The ache of losing Gabe reasserted itself, pressing in on all sides until she let out a small moan.

"What's wrong?" Michael asked.

Keely shook her head, but it was no use. Tears stung her eyes. "I was just remembering you, me, and Gabe in the mall."

He stared off into the distance, a look of pain spreading slowly across his face. "Yeah," he mumbled, lifting his glass. "Gabe would have approved of this."

Keely let her head drop against her chest. She missed Gabe. She knew Michael missed him too, that they were both hurting over Gabe's death, both feeling shades of responsibility, guilt, remorse.

She wanted to talk about it but couldn't get past the painful lump in her throat. Besides, what would they say? It all sounded trite. After Strain 7, deaths were commonplace. It wasn't supposed to be a big deal anymore. Life was supposed to be cheaper, not so important.

At least, that was one theory.

"We should get the others," Keely said.

"We should," Michael agreed. "But somehow I'm having trouble getting motivated."

"I've noticed," she said, turning to him. "Where have you been, Michael? This whole trip I feel like we lost a part of you along the way."

Michael snorted. "Yeah? What part of me? The part that played fetch for Slattery and brought the electric fence technology and GPS disks to Novo Mundum? Good riddance. I hope that part's dead and buried."

"I was on that mission too," she said. "We all believed in Novo Mundum. Gabe too. So should we throw ourselves off the next cliff?"

He lifted his glass. "Sure. Why not?"

"My point here: Don't quit trying to do what's right, Michael."

"But that's just it," he said, glancing up at her. "I wouldn't know the right thing if it bit me on the ass."

As Keely looked into his haunted, hollow stare, she suddenly recognized something. She'd seen that exact expression before—on her mother.

Was that what happened to her? Keely wondered. *Did she try to do good, only to have the lines between good and bad blur?*

"Just help the people closest to you. You don't have to save the whole world."

Keely whispered the words before she realized how much they applied to her too. In fact, it should have been the mantra of their whole group, so busy trying to save friends and family in Novo Mundum. Crossing through a blizzard, trying to be heroes. And for what? She lifted her glass and took a long sip. They would probably get killed in the process.

TWENTY-SEVEN

Diego tiptoed down the wide staircase in the lake resort's main building, pushed open the door, and stepped outside.

The night was beautiful. It was freezing, but the sky was clear for the first time in days. A thin sliver of moon was rising above the pines, and thousands of tiny stars winked at him. Holding his bow tightly, Diego trudged uphill to the dark forest and slipped in among the trees.

He had only gone a few yards when he heard a noise behind him—the unmistakable rhythm of two-legged footfalls. He whirled around and aimed his bow.

"Don't shoot," said the slender figure, lifting her arms into the air. "It's just me." She stepped forward out of the shadows.

"Liza?" Diego lowered his bow. "What are you doing here?"

"I couldn't sleep." She tucked her hands into her pockets. "So . . . what are you doing?"

"Hunting. I found a game trail when we were out here earlier and I want to try and get us some food."

"Can I come with you?"

There was something in her manner that he recognized, something he himself possessed—a restlessness that drove people either into the wilderness or out of their minds. "Moonstruck," his nonnie called it. He'd had it all his life.

"Okay," he said.

She fell into step beside him and the two of them quietly tramped through the powdery snow.

"Why can't you sleep?" he asked as the silence grew awkward.

Liza's features twisted into a grimace. "I keep having bad dreams."

"About what?"

"My father." Her face hardened even more. "It's not fair. When I'm awake, I can't stop thinking about everything he did and how much I hate him. And now it happens when I'm asleep. I can't get away from him."

"I know what you mean," Diego muttered. "No offense, but I hate your father too. We all do."

"Not Michael. He says he does, but really he hates himself."

Diego studied her scowling profile. Before their escape, he had barely spent any time with Liza, knowing her mainly as "Slattery's daughter" or "Michael's new squeeze." And she'd always struck him as rather soft, unnaturally preserved from the harshness of the world, but that wasn't completely accurate.

"It's such a waste," she went on. "Michael should be mad at the people who really deserve it instead of punishing himself."

Diego nodded. "We all deal in different ways," he remarked, trying to appear neutral.

"Yeah, some of us in sicker ways than others."

Diego stopped walking and turned toward her. "What's that about?" When she hesitated, he prodded her. "You can tell me."

She took a breath. "There's only one thing that helps for me. Sometimes I have these daydreams about . . . about killing my father." She gazed cautiously at Diego, gauging his reaction. "It's awful, I know. It's sick and twisted and totally—"

"But it makes you feel a little better, doesn't it?" Diego broke in.

She nodded.

"You're pissed and you want to do something with all those feelings. I get that. And it's not like there are any rules on how to deal with this sort of crap. What are you supposed to do? Roll over and accept it?" He shook his head. "Screw that. If thinking those things is what keeps you going, then I say go for it."

She seemed to soak in his answer as they walked along. Suddenly she turned to him. "Can I ask you a question? Do you like me?"

"I haven't known you that long," he said diplomatically. "But honestly, you've handled this whole trip with a good attitude."

"And the others? If you haven't noticed, I'm not exactly the best of friends with Keely and Irene."

"Don't take it personally. We all grew really close on our journey to Novo Mundum."

"So how come that isn't happening now?"

Diego didn't answer. She was right. They weren't bonding. If anything, their group was slowly coming apart.

"Is it me?" Liza asked. "Am I, like, the bad seed, ruining the crop? Because I'm not that way. Not spoiled, the way people think. Sheltered, yes. But I have a mind of my own."

"I can see that," he teased, though he knew where she was coming from. Diego had grown up with plenty of freedom, something that was impossible to surrender.

"I'm probably talking too much." She frowned. "It's just that Michael hasn't been up for much conversation."

Don't want to go there, Diego thought, surprised at how much Liza was opening up. He was relieved that they had come to a small, moonlit clearing.

"There's the trail," he whispered. "Let's find cover. A lot of animals have better night vision than we do." He led her to a fallen tree nearby and the two of them crouched down behind the gnarled mass of roots. The close proximity unnerved him, and he could feel Liza's eyes on him as he readied an arrow and propped his bow on the log.

"Thanks, Diego," she said softly.

He kept his eyes on his bow. "For what?"

"For everything. Helping me. Stepping up and taking care of our group. You know, we couldn't have made it without you."

"No problem." He had to admit, it was nice to be acknowledged. He just wished those words had come from Irene.

TWENTY-EIGHT

THE SUN WAS BACK. IT WARMED IRENE'S SPIRITS AND illuminated ice crystals in the snow, making the world shimmer. Unfortunately, it also melted the snow, which refroze overnight, making their hike icy and treacherous. Still, the constant cloud cover had been making her feel claustrophobic, and she welcomed the new weather. In fact, it was probably the one bright spot at the moment.

Their brief stay at the ramshackle resort had been a refreshing break, but sleeping on a mattress again (even a musty, mouse-chewed one) only made the ground feel harder the next night. Soon after they left, a pall settled over the group. Their faces showed the strain, and they moved with little or no conversation.

The stress, combined with the monotonous travel on foot, was wearing down nerves.

They were scrambling through an icy ravine when Liza suddenly slipped and fell forward. Diego quickly responded, helping her to her feet with an exchange that implied some sort of understanding, even a friendship. When had that happened?

Irene frowned. *Quit being silly,* she told herself as they resumed hiking. *It was nothing. Nothing at all.*

In the middle of the night she'd woken to find Diego not in bed. That in itself wasn't unusual since he often got up to take watch or hunt or pace restlessly. But then she'd noticed Liza was missing too. At the time Irene had assumed Liza went for a bathroom break. Irene had probably assumed wrong, because today it was clear that the relationship dynamic between Liza and Diego had shifted. Liza tagged along close behind him, and Diego didn't seem to mind. That alone shouldn't have bothered Irene, but it did.

Is something going on between them?

"Everyone stop." Diego came to a halt and turned to face them. "Look up there." He gestured to a rocky ledge at the top of the nearby hill.

Irene squinted up, but she couldn't see anything. Just a group of granite-streaked boulders thrusting out of the hilltop surrounded by a few droopy oaks.

"What is it?" she asked.

"A cave. Don't you see it?" He extended his forefinger and jabbed at the air, indicating the westernmost point. Sure enough, Irene could make out a triangle of darkness that suggested an opening in the rocks. "We should stop and make camp there."

Irene stopped herself from saying, "Already?" It was only the middle of the afternoon and Diego usually wanted them to continue until dusk. "It can't be much past noon."

Diego grinned, amused by their surprise. "Come on. We need extra time if we want to do something special to celebrate."

Celebrate what? Irene glanced over at Michael, who looked just as confused as she felt.

Now Diego looked annoyed. "You do know what day it is, don't you?"

It was Keely who spoke up. "Thanksgiving."

Irene thought back, trying to track the days since they'd left Novo Mundum, but all she could remember was a panicky blur of snow and trees and achy joints.

"You're right," Liza said. She too seemed to be counting the days off on her fingers. "Today's Thanksgiving."

Diego shook his head, as if amused by their stupidity. "I'm going to go check it out and make sure it's safe. Then we'll treat ourselves to a feast."

"I'll go with you," Liza said.

Irene bit her lip as the two of them ascended the rocky hill. *There's nothing to worry about,* she told herself.

Irene inhaled the heady mix of aromas. The plump pheasant Diego had shot was roasting on the makeshift spit. The chestnuts they'd gathered were sizzling on the hot rocks, and a pot they'd scavenged from the resort for boiling water was now stuffed with edible greens she and Keely had harvested per Diego's instructions. The cave had become a somewhat hospitable gathering place, its musty walls dappled with golden light. There were even "plates"—real, porcelain plates Diego had secretly lugged from the resort. Irene shook her head in amazement. He had thought of everything.

She stirred the pot of greens and bent down to take a whiff. It smelled, well, *green*—even though the leaves themselves had boiled down to a more grayish color. She knew animals ate them and survived, and Diego said he'd had them a few times when he was by himself and the hunting wasn't so good. But she would probably only have a bite or two, just to be polite.

Diego lifted the bird off the fire and began carving it carefully. "That's it. Everyone dig in."

They each took a plate, loaded it with food, and sat down in a circle around the fire, glancing at one another as if waiting for something.

"Do you think one of us should, maybe, say something?" Keely asked. "I mean, since it is a special occasion?"

Everyone looked at Diego.

"Yeah, sure. I'll do it," he said. He bowed his head. "We give thanks for this food, this shelter, and that we've managed to stay out of harm's way and carry on in these difficult times. May our bellies continue to be full, the forest continue to hide us, and our enemies continue to stay far away."

"Amen," everyone echoed.

"Okay, let's eat."

For a while everyone ate in comfortable silence. The pheasant and chestnuts had both been roasted to perfection. Even the greens were tasty in a plain, organic sort of way. If they'd had a pinch of salt, they'd have actually been quite good.

Irene looked over at Diego, his handsome profile mottled by firelight. It was strange how even though he was right next to her, she missed him. It seemed like forever since they'd really, truly connected. There was that near moment on the summit, when everything went from wonderful to horrible in an instant. She'd been wanting to talk to him about it—to apologize and explain herself—but had just never had the chance.

But this was it—her moment to tell him how sincerely grateful she felt for this interlude of near normalcy in the middle of their crazy journey. She knew those words would be a step toward mending things between them.

She was just about to reach for Diego's hand when Liza piped up. "Thanks, Diego," she said. "For the food. For everything."

The others added their own words of gratitude. Irene chimed in, silently frustrated that the gesture had been stolen from her.

Diego shrugged. "Yeah, well, Thanksgiving was always a big deal at home."

"Really?" Keely asked through a mouthful of chestnut. "What was it like?"

He stared into the distance, remembering. "Well, we didn't have turkey usually. Instead Nonnie used to make piles of tamales and a big pot of *carne guisada*. My uncle Gilbert would bring his guitar and we would all sing songs. Then after the little ones went to bed, we'd stay up late playing poker. Nonnie always creamed us. Of course, I think she cheated a little, too." He shook his head and smiled.

"Sounds wonderful," Irene said. "We always had turkey. And Aaron and I would fight over the wishbone. Seems so silly now." She closed her eyes and recalled their dining room table set with the good china, her grandmother's lace tablecloth, and the floppy, cardboard cornucopia she'd made in fourth grade that always served as their centerpiece. What had happened to that thing?

Keely laughed softly. "My most vivid memory is of being in a terrible elementary school play about the first Thanksgiving. I had to dress up as this Indian princess and bring an armload of corn to the Pilgrims. Only the real corn I was supposed to carry had all these bugs crawling on it and I ended up just throwing it onto the stage and running away."

Everyone laughed.

"Yep. The beginning and end of my theater career," Keely said. She turned to her left. "What about you, Michael? What were your Thanksgivings like?"

Michael sat for a long moment staring at the fire. Irene was beginning to think he would never answer when suddenly he smiled. "I remember my mom's pies," he murmured. "She made the best pecan pies ever—with just a little hint of rum."

A small chorus of *mmm*'s welled up from the group.

"What about you, Liza?" Irene asked.

Liza's brow puckered. "I don't want to talk about this," she said quietly. "I don't want to think about my family."

Irene tensed as she and Keely exchanged an uncomfortable glance, Michael's eyes glazing over once again.

Keely reached across Michael to pat Liza on the arm. "We understand. It's hard."

"No, you *don't* understand." Liza's voice cracked with emotion, but she held her head high. "You guys have lost people you loved. Well, I didn't lose my dad and uncle. I lost *me*—my life, the one I thought I had!" She slammed down her plate and scrambled to her feet. "I *wish* they had died!"

Everyone watched in awkward silence as she stomped to the cave entrance.

Keely prodded Michael. "Go talk to her. Tell her it's going to be okay."

He shook his head. "I can't promise her that. How do I know everything's going to be okay? What if it isn't? What if it gets worse?"

Irene gaped at him. She would have never thought Michael could sound so uncaring. "What is wrong with you?" she demanded.

"What's wrong with any of us?" he snapped. "It's a messed-up world, and Liza has a right to feel bad. I don't think it's fair to fill her head with false hopes."

"I'll go talk to her." Diego rose to his feet and limped to the mouth of the cave.

Irene's chest tightened as she watched him place a

hand on Liza's back and lean over her hunched, sobbing form, talking to her in hushed tones. She was glad Diego was good enough to take on what Michael should be doing, but somehow it hurt her, too.

After all, she'd needed comfort these past several days. Why hadn't he been there for her?

TWENTY-NINE

LIZA SAT UP AND RUBBED HER EYES, HER HANDS STILL WEAK and floppy from sleep. A scene of quiet activity slowly came into focus around her. The others were bustling about, rolling up bedrolls and stuffing supplies inside their packs. Beyond the narrow opening of the cave gray sunlight strained through clay-colored clouds.

So it wasn't just a bad dream. She was still in the middle of nowhere, her father was still a murderer, and she was still on the run. She shivered, pulling her blanket up to her shoulders. Although she knew she'd need to get up in a minute, she didn't want reality, didn't want to face Michael's beaten expression. She knew that he too was in the middle of his own living nightmare.

If only she could go back to sleep and pretend it wasn't happening.

"Leave your gun for the others. We won't be needing it."

"What about the knife?"

"Yeah. Bring the knife."

Liza turned toward the voices—Diego and Michael. Her mood lifted to see Diego, the only person who totally got her and understood what she was dealing with.

She watched him as he left Michael and walked over to Irene and Keely, his longbow resting on one shoulder. "I'm going to check the trap, see if I can snag some food before we leave."

"But we're almost in the St. Louis suburbs," Irene said. "Just a few more miles and we should be in the next town."

"Exactly why I want to go," Diego explained. "Hunting will be better in the forest. You know the towns are picked over as far as food is concerned."

Liza struggled out of her sleeping bag and loped over to them. "I'll go with you," she said to Diego.

She so needed this right now. The time she'd gone hunting with Diego had been the least insane part of this torturous journey. If she could just have another moment of peace, she might be able to make it the rest of the way without completely checking out.

Diego shook his head. "That's okay, Liza. Michael's coming and that's all the help I need. You guys stay here and take down camp."

A wave of disappointment swept over her. She really didn't want to stay behind. Not with Keely and Irene.

They'd never really let her into their friendship, and he knew that too. Surely he could sense how much she needed this.

"But I want to go with you guys." Liza could see Irene and Keely exchange looks. So what if she sounded like a bratty nine-year-old? "I can help. Really. Please, Diego?"

"Thanks, but three would be too many. We won't be long." Diego headed toward the mouth of the cave, where Michael was already waiting. "Try and erase all traces of our camp," he called out over his shoulder. "We don't want anyone to know we came this way."

Liza stood rooted to her spot until Diego and Michael disappeared from sight. Keely and Irene had already sprung into action, covering up the fire pit with a thick layer of dirt.

"I hope he doesn't stay out long," Irene muttered to Keely. "Did you see how stiff he was this morning? I wish he'd take it easy—just for one day."

Keely nodded sympathetically.

A jet of anger suddenly shot up inside Liza and she whirled around, glaring at Irene. "What is with you?" she snapped.

Irene and Keely blinked in confusion.

"What? Me?" Irene asked.

"Why are you always so hard on Diego?" Liza demanded.

Irene continued to gape at her. "I'm not hard on him. I'm just worried about him," she replied in a slow, deliberate voice. "He was shot in the leg by a soldier not that long ago. He almost died, Liza. It's not the sort of injury you can ignore for long."

Liza shook her head. "You're only making it tougher for him. He's busting his butt trying to take care of us, and all you do is nag him."

"You're right—he *is* busting his butt." Irene's voice rose to match Liza's shrill pitch. "And if he ends up hurting himself, he's not going to be able to help anyone."

Keely placed one hand on Irene's shoulder and held the other out toward Liza. "Guys, calm down."

Liza ignored her. "Diego knows what he's doing," she said. "He's lived like this before."

"*And* he's gotten hurt before," Irene countered.

"Guys," Keely warned. "Let's cut this out. Not worth arguing about it."

But Liza had unleashed too much frustration to start reining it in. She couldn't stand to hear Diego criticized after everything he'd done for her. And she really, *really* didn't like being lectured.

"I'm not stupid," she muttered through her teeth. "You don't have to talk to me like I'm an idiot."

"I'm not," Irene said. She stared at Liza, her face softening into a worried expression that Liza couldn't bear. "Look, Diego is trying to prove something to himself. He's angry and he isn't thinking straight. I'm just trying to get him to—"

"What's wrong with being angry?" Liza interrupted. "He *should* be angry! You guys don't know what it's like. At least you have people out there somewhere. Michael too. But Diego's family is all dead. And mine are as good as dead." Liza's voice cracked with emotion, which only made her angrier. She clenched her fists and kicked the end of her sleeping bag. "Don't you get it? We have nobody."

"We have each other," Irene said softly.

Liza bristled at her sympathy. "That's not the same and you know it. We—"

She stopped as the light in the cave suddenly dimmed. She turned and saw an enormous shape silhouetted against the mouth of the cave. In a quick, fluid motion it slunk through the opening and into the dim light.

Oh my God! she thought as her anger gave way to terror. It was almost too absurd for her brain to grasp.

A tiger.

A real live tiger was standing directly in front of her, its yellow eyes staring right into hers.

THIRTY

A HIGH-PITCHED SCREAM TORE THROUGH THE AIR.

"What the hell?" Diego glanced over at Michael.

"That's Liza," he said, his face turning pale.

The two turned and charged through the trees, racing back up the slope toward the cave.

Michael reached it a second before he did. Diego could see him come to a sudden halt, as if he'd hit some sort of invisible barrier. "Holy crap," he exclaimed, his eyes wide.

Then Diego ran inside. He too skidded to a stop, frozen with shock at the scene before him. Liza was huddled against the cave wall, shaking with panic. And slowly stalking toward her was a grown tiger. Its ears were flattened against its large head and its mouth was partially open to reveal several sharp, saliva-coated teeth.

"Liza, stay still!" Keely shouted from the back of the cave, where she and Irene stood gripping each other. "Try not to move!"

The tiger continued its slow, steady creep toward Liza, seeming oblivious to the rest of them. It looked thin for such a large animal, and its fur was pocked with various nicks and scrapes. Around its neck was a black electronic-looking gadget, like a radio-controlled collar. But there was no mistaking its powerful jaws. It could still kill.

Michael swiped desperately at his left hip and then turned toward Diego with a frantic expression. "I don't have my gun," he said. He glanced nervously at the dark mound of his backpack, which the tiger was now skirting past. The gun belt lay beside it.

Right. Diego remembered telling him to leave it behind when they went hunting.

They had to do something fast. The tiger was crouching lower, its tail twitching rhythmically. Diego raised his bow and took careful aim, knowing he'd probably only get one shot. Taking a deep breath, he steadied his grip and let the arrow fly. . . .

There came a faint whipping sound followed by a dull *thunk,* and the tiger instantly fell sideways, an arrow stuck through its neck. It twitched and flailed for a second, letting out a series of guttural hacking sounds, until finally it lay still.

Diego exhaled in relief. Liza let out another cry and collapsed to the ground.

"Nice shot," came a voice from behind.

Diego spun around. Two men were standing in the cave entrance. One was large and burly, with a bullet-shaped bald head and a thick brown mustache. The other was thinner, with long, graying blond hair and a wind-chapped face. Both men were dressed in dark, metal-studded leather and had long diagonal scars across their right cheeks.

A chill skittered down Diego's spine. *The Slash.*

He reached for a new arrow, but the big guy locked his automatic and pointed it right at his head. "Don't even think about it," he said menacingly.

The other guy snickered. He grabbed Diego's bow and quiver and yanked them off him.

Now what? Diego looked at Michael, at Liza crumpled and crying on the floor of the cave, Keely and Irene huddled together in horror. He'd let them down. He had insisted on going hunting that morning instead of leaving. He had arranged the huge feast the night before, the scent of which probably attracted the tiger. It was all his fault.

Just then another man came charging into the cave. He also had a slanting stripe cut into his cheek and the same freckled, weather-beaten face as the long-haired guy but shorter hair and a stockier build.

He pushed past the other two men and ran straight up to the tiger. "Bubba?" he said in a deep yet almost childlike voice. He nudged the dead beast a few times and then stared at his hand in horror. It glistened bright red. The man let out a whimper and his round face darkened. "Bubba!" he howled, bursting into tears.

"He's dead, Lester," the long-haired guy said casually. "This guy killed him with one shot." He gestured toward Diego with the barrel of his gun.

Lester grunted in rage and lunged at Diego. "You killed him! You killed my Bubba!" He got in Diego's face, so close Diego could see the tiny bloodshot veins in his cheeks. "Now I'm going to kill you!"

"Wait! Stop, Lester." The long-haired guy stepped in between them and held the stocky guy by his shoulders. "It's all right," he said consolingly. "The chief's gonna be really happy with us. We're gonna bring him a hunter and a bunch of pretty women. He'll be so happy, he'll probably give you a new pet."

"A elephant?" Lester asked hopefully, turning away from Diego.

"Maybe."

"I want a elephant, Roscoe!"

"Hyper down, Lester. Roscoe, get your brother to keep still," the biggest guy ordered. "We gotta load up our valuable finds here and take them back to headquarters."

Roscoe, the long-haired brute, smiled viciously at Diego. "Yes, sirree. Thanks to you, I'm gonna get to party tonight." He threw back his straggly mane and cackled. Lester joined in, oblivious to why they were laughing.

Not again, Diego thought as he was pushed against the wall of the cave. *No way am I going to be kept captive again.*

THIRTY-ONE

LIZA SLUMPED IN THE BACK CORNER OF THE FLATBED TRUCK, her hands tied behind her back. Her shoulders ached from straining against the bindings, and she had cried so much since the episode with the tiger, her entire face felt swollen and bruised.

Beside her, Roscoe sat on a low built-in bench, holding his gun at the ready. To his left, Irene sat slouched, her face hidden behind a curtain of dark curls. Diego and Michael sat across from them on the opposite bench, and Keely rode in the cab with the big guy, who was driving.

Lester sat like a freckled Buddha in the middle of the truck bed, still sobbing and mumbling to himself. "Bubba was a good tiger. I trained him good. He hunted for us."

"That tiger wasn't no good hunter," Roscoe retorted, then leaned his head over the truck rail and spat onto the road below. He'd tried to comfort his brother throughout the drive, to no avail. Now he seemed to be growing more and more irritated. "He ate up every damn thing he caught and wouldn't leave us nothing," he went on. "Or he'd leave us a mangled mess that wasn't no good to eat anyways. But this boy . . ." Roscoe grinned menacingly at Diego, who sat slouched on the bench across from him. "He's a little gimpy, but this boy could get us some prime stuff. I bet you can nab deer and rabbits and stuff with that bow you got, huh?"

Diego refused to answer, refused to even look at him.

"No! He won't be good," Lester said with a pout. "I don't like him. He killed Bubba."

Roscoe looked sadly at his brother. Then he lifted his foot and kicked Diego with the toe of his boot. "I know what you're thinking. He acts like a big baby, I know. Been that way since the motorcycle accident." He turned and spat again, his eyes distant. "But he's one mean mother, and you did kill his pet. If I were you, I'd say sorry."

"Go to hell!" Diego said, with restrained anger. "Both of you."

Roscoe sat forward, a sudden homicidal glint in his squinty eyes. Liza braced herself for Diego's swift retribution, either from Roscoe's boot or fist or worse—like the gun he held across his lap. But before he could do anything, Irene stumbled forward and leaned in between them.

"We're sorry!" she cried, shooting Roscoe a pleading look. Then she turned toward Lester. "Sorry, Lester. We're so sorry we killed Bubba."

Lester just sat there, breathing heavily and glaring down at his lap. Suddenly his face twisted in a wretched grimace and his hand flew up, whacking Irene across the face and sending her sprawling backward against the floor of the truck. "Shut up!" he yelled, sobbing again.

Diego let out a grunt of rage and threw himself on Lester, butting him with his head and kicking out with his knees.

Roscoe jumped to his feet. "Get off my brother!" he hollered, kicking Diego in the ribs. Diego kept right on raging. Lester was shielding his head and yelling, Irene was shouting something, and Liza suddenly realized that she too was screaming.

"I said"—Liza winced as she saw Roscoe raise his rifle—"get off my brother!" he finished yelling, slamming the butt of the gun against Diego's skull.

Diego fell back, clutching his head and twisting slowly from side to side. Lester crawled away, whimpering.

"Oh my God, oh my God," Irene chanted, scooting up beside Diego.

Roscoe slumped back down on the bench, his rage apparently spent. "You guys sure are a lively bunch," he mused, spitting over the side again. "It's okay, Lester," he said to his brother, who was rocking himself back and forth, sniveling loudly and wiping his nose on his sleeve. "Why don't you pick yourself out a woman? You found 'em, so you get to keep one."

"No!" Lester shook his head vigorously. "I want a elephant."

"Whatever," Roscoe said with a shrug. "Me? I like this one here." Liza cringed as he leaned sideways and reached his hand out toward her, grasping a lock of her hair. "Always did like redheads."

"Get your slimy paws off her!" Michael suddenly yelled, staggering toward him.

"What did you say?"

Liza recognized the murderous gleam in Roscoe's eyes. "Michael, don't," she pleaded.

"I said leave her alone!" Michael said, meeting his glare.

"Oh? She yours? Is that it?" Roscoe asked. "Think you're better than me, huh? Real ladies' man? Well, that's about to change, asshole. Lots of things are gonna change." He slung the rifle over his shoulder, pulled a switchblade out of his back pocket, and flipped it open. "Hold him down, Lester."

"No!" Liza and Irene both yelled.

Lester glanced up excitedly. He crawled over to Michael and pinned him back against the side of the truck with his own girth. "I got him, Roscoe," he said, his voice high and eager. "I got him! I got him!"

"Good boy, Lester," Roscoe muttered.

Liza watched in horror as Roscoe knelt down beside Michael, pressed the tip of the blade beside his right eye, and began slicing downward at an angle. Michael screamed in agony.

"Stop it! Please, stop!" Liza screamed, squirming as she saw a rivulet of blood stream down Michael's face.

A few seconds later Roscoe leaned back and lowered the knife. "Yeah!" he cried triumphantly. He stepped back to admire his work: A bloody gash divided Michael's cheek. "Now who's the man?"

A slash—the gang symbol.

A bitter taste filled Liza's mouth. *This can't be happening,* she thought, closing her eyes. Just that morning she'd been comparing her life to a nightmare; now she'd give anything to go back to that time.

Suddenly the truck came to a screeching halt and Liza was tossed forward against the bench. The driver door opened and the big bald guy leaned out. "What the hell is going on back there?" he demanded, his mustache framing his down-turned lips. Liza could see Keely's wide, anxious-looking eyes through the cab's dirt-streaked windshield.

"Nothing we can't handle, Dozer," Roscoe replied. "A couple of these guys got a little cocky about their women, so we had to put them in their place."

The big guy's bleary eyes glanced from Diego's sprawled, half-conscious form to Michael, panting and bleeding in his seat.

"Fine, but take it easy with the female merchandise. The Commander gets first dibs, and you know he doesn't like it if they come in damaged," he instructed. "If you behave, he'll let you keep one as a prize—*after* he's done with them."

He ducked back into the cab and revved the engine again.

Roscoe muttered something under his breath and then glanced at Liza. "Don't worry," he said with a wink. "I'll get you later, doll."

THIRTY-TWO

KEELY SHUDDERED AS THE TRUCK ROLLED THROUGH A BRICK arch—the entrance of the Slash compound in St. Louis. What the place had once been, she couldn't yet tell, but it seemed to have a few acres of grounds as well as paved walkways and dry fountains. The sign on the gate had been disassembled, preserving only the sideways-leaning strokes of letters to create a long row of slash marks.

The big bald guy, or Dozer, as he called himself, pulled into a small paved lot and parked the pickup among a collection of vehicles—cars, trucks, campers, even an old-fashioned buggy. Most were in various states of repair. Some had lost tires or doors or had whole engines missing from beneath their raised hoods. In the post–Strain 7 world it was surprising to see so many cars, even if they did seem pieced together.

"Get out." Dozer reached across to open the passenger-side door, then pointed his revolver toward Keely. "And no funny business. I'd hate to have to hurt you, blondie, before I even get the chance to know you better."

Keely climbed out and waited as the others clambered from the back, stumbling awkwardly with their hands still bound behind them.

"All right, get going," Dozer ordered, prodding her with the barrel of his gun. "You lead them in, Roscoe. I'll stay and watch from behind."

Roscoe and Lester started along a gravel path. Diego staggered after them. His head was raised stoically, almost proudly, and his eyes were angry slits. After him went Irene, who looked okay except for a red streak along the left side of her face, then Liza, who seemed scared as hell but otherwise all right. Michael looked by far the worst. His cheek was a mess of dried blood and swollen skin and he seemed ready to pass out from the pain. Keely took up the rear, overly aware of Dozer's scrunching footsteps behind her.

As they walked, Keely could hear strange screeching noises in the distance, and an acrid, barnyard-like smell grew more and more powerful. The trail meandered through a dense patch of bamboo and then opened into a wide, cobbled courtyard, bustling with activity. The scene was completely surreal. There were men riding camels and ostriches. An elephant lumbered by on a chain leash, several large boxes tied to his back. And in the middle of the expanse was a giant wrought-iron cage full of chattering monkeys.

A zoo! she thought. *So that's how they got a tiger.*

It occurred to her that she'd never really wondered about the zoos before. She knew they'd all been closed, but she hadn't given much thought to what had become of the animals. Perhaps MacCauley's soldiers had sent everyone away from here, leaving the animals to fend for themselves. Or maybe a few loyal keepers had stayed behind, only to fall dead from Strain 7—or at the hands of the Slash.

They crossed the courtyard and headed onto a sloping brick path, passing rows of cages on both sides. Keely was surprised to see there were still several animals alive, if not exactly healthy and well cared for. A couple of squawking parrots, a drowsy-looking brown bear, and a group of kangaroos glanced up as they walked past. There were even a few animals roaming free. Keely spotted a three-toed sloth hanging from a tree branch, and a few men walked around with live monkeys or birds on their shoulders.

The rest of the Slash seemed just as scary and sanity challenged as their guys. The compound was overwhelmingly mostly men, with barely any women. Not all of them were big, but they all looked tough. Almost everyone wore leather with a few little embellishments that seemed to denote rank, like bits of fur or the skins of exotic reptiles. As Keely and the others passed, the men would stop what they were doing and leer at them, shouting out filthy come-ons to the girls and words of congratulations to Roscoe, Dozer, and Lester.

"Got some live ones, huh?"

"Hey, baby, wanna go in the snake house with me?"

As scared as she was, there was also a small part of Keely—no doubt the dorky scientist part she'd inherited from her mother—that marveled at the Slash's crude yet effective government. Overall, they appeared to have a relatively functional headquarters. And judging by some of the things Dozer had said about the Commander during the drive, it was clear they had firm rules and a system of rewards. But any amazement she felt was tempered by the main, horrifying truth—this group of men bonded over their shared love of crime and torture, and she was their "guest."

Liza had slowed considerably, dropping back to the spot in front of Keely. Suddenly she froze in place, and Keely almost knocked her flat.

"Keep moving!" Dozer ordered. Again Keely felt his gun poke her in the back.

She positioned herself right behind Liza, trying to prod her with her shoulder. "It's okay," she whispered. "Just do what they tell us."

Liza began walking tentatively again. "But look!" she whispered. "Look up ahead."

They were coming up on a group of people huddled inside a large cage, about six or seven in all: an older woman, three young male soldiers, and a couple of elderly men. Like the animals, they all looked half starved. As their group walked past, one of the older men in the cage rose shakily to his feet and began shouting gibberish at them, prompting a thuggish guard to jab him with a stick until he grew quiet.

"Is that what they're going to do to us?" Liza asked.

"I don't know," Keely replied.

Dozer chuckled behind them. "You want to see what could happen to you? Do you?" He cupped one hand around his mouth. "Roscoe! Take them by the pits!"

Roscoe and Lester started to laugh. They veered to the right and led them to a deep, circular enclosure surrounded by a low wrought-iron fence.

"Look down!" Dozer ordered. He and Roscoe pushed everyone forward until they were slammed against the iron rails. Knowing she didn't want to, Keely glanced down.

Several full-grown alligators swam in a pool of murky water. Strewn throughout the sandy embankment was a gruesome debris of human skulls, bits of bone, and several pieces of torn, blood-soaked clothing.

Liza made a strange gargling sound. Then she doubled over the rails and retched into the pit, causing the alligators to snap and thrash.

Roscoe, Lester, and Dozer laughed maniacally.

"See that?" Dozer said. "That will be your new home *if* you don't behave."

So this is the guy? Keely thought.

They were standing in a darkened theater that served as some sort of governing hall for the Slash. On the stage before them sat the Commander, lit up by a semicircle of makeshift torches.

She'd expected him to be the biggest, meanest-looking Slash of all. Instead the man was older and even a little smaller than most of the others. To Keely he resembled a twisted, Harley-Davidson Santa Claus. He sat on a high-backed chair draped with animal skins, including one with an attached lion's head that loomed over the top of the seat back. He had a dark ponytail peppered with gray, a bushy mustache, and a long beard that seemed to be made out of gray fuzz instead of hair. His black leather racing jacket was heavily decorated with metal studs and sharp, curved pieces that looked like animal tusks and teeth. And all around him stood pretty young women in various stages of undress. Some had on leather, some shivered in lingerie. All of them wore the same empty, shell-shocked expression.

"Roscoe. Dozer. Lester," the Commander muttered, greeting each man with a nod. "How did your hunting expedition go this time? Where's Bubba?"

"Dead!" Lester wailed. He broke into a fresh round of sobs and jabbed his index finger toward Diego. "He killed him!"

"Keep your brother quiet, Roscoe."

"Sorry, Commander." Roscoe reached over and grabbed Lester by the scruff of his T-shirt. "I told you to be quiet," he said in a panicky whisper. "Remember what I said? If you want to stay here with me, you got to be quiet around the chief. Got it?"

Lester nodded silently, his lower lip jutted forward and trembling.

Dozer went on. "Bubba led us to a cave. We thought he was on an animal scent, but instead he tracked this group of people camping. When we caught up with him, Bubba was going after one of them, and this guy here"—he pointed at Diego—"he killed that damn tiger with one shot from his bow and arrow."

"One shot?" The Commander looked skeptical.

"Yep, he did," Roscoe chimed in. "We saw it with our own eyes. We lost Bubba, but we found ourselves a real hunter. He could get us meat much better than that stupid trained tiger."

Diego suddenly lurched out of Roscoe's grasp. "No goddamn way!" he yelled.

"Shut your ass up and show some respect!" Roscoe shouted, pulling him back and whacking the side of his head. "This here's the Commander!" He looked back at the man on the throne, grinning apologetically. "Course, he's a real hothead, too."

The Commander frowned. "That could be a problem." He leaned forward and glared down at Diego. "You should keep yourself in line, asshole, if you know what's good for you. Our canned food stores are damn near empty and these knuckleheads are good at killing but crap at hunting. Your skill will keep you alive as long as you behave. Otherwise I'll be more than happy to introduce you to a few of my alligator friends." He sat back and crossed his beefy arms across his chest. "What about the others?"

Dozer shoved Michael forward. It broke Keely's heart to see him swaying in front of the Commander, his muscles twitching from anger and pain. "This one here is young and strong," Dozer said, thumping Michael on the back, "but he also needs to learn some manners. Roscoe had to brand the shithead on the way over."

The Commander looked him over and grunted a halfhearted approval. "What else?" he said, squinting into the darkness.

"Commander," Dozer began in his most reverent tone. "We are also happy to present you with these three fine women."

He and Roscoe grabbed Keely, Liza, and Irene and yanked them into the light. The Commander let out a long, low whistle. *"Mmm,"* he said, rubbing his frizzy beard and looking each of them up and down. "You've done well. In fact, I'd say we need to break out the bottles and celebrate your little haul."

"Yes!" Roscoe whispered behind Keely.

"After the party I'll look over the females," the Commander continued. "When I'm finished, you'll each get one for yourself to keep as long as you need or trade if you wish. I'll decide what to do about the men later. But first"—he rose to his feet and pumped his fist in the air—"bring out the booze!"

Roscoe, Dozer, and a few other guards in the room erupted in cheers.

The Commander glanced about. "Where's my queen?" he hollered. "Fetch me my queen!"

Someone ran off behind the stage. Soon after, a

teenage girl stepped out of the wings dressed in leather chap pants and a metal-studded leather halter. Keely gasped. *It couldn't be.* Long pale blond hair, big lost-looking eyes . . .

Maggie?

THIRTY-THREE

MICHAEL MOANED AND STRAINED AT THE METAL CUFFS CLAMPING his wrists. It was colder down here in what they referred to as the "dungeon." The room was actually a dank, dusty storage cellar outfitted with heavy iron chains and shackles—the kind used on large beasts. He tried to remember how they'd gotten down there, but it was all just a heady blur, like a nightmare on fast-forward.

Yet amid the chaos and confusion and blinding pain, Michael had been aware of one overriding thought: *Maggie was here!* For weeks he'd figured she must be dead. Starved or shot by soldiers. Ravaged by sickness and exposure. But never, ever had he imagined a form of torture like this.

Another mistake on his head: he should have stopped her. He could have stayed behind while the others went on and combed the area until he'd found her. Instead he'd given up. In fact, to be honest, he'd been relieved not to be burdened with her anymore. And now look at her. How horrible her life must be, all because of his selfishness. And the fact that Liza, Keely, and Irene would soon suffer the same fate was a thought too horrible to bear.

He glanced around the room at the others. Keely was staring off into space, looking lost. Liza was quietly crying. And Irene was talking in a shaky whisper to Diego, who was cursing and pulling at his irons. Michael had to rotate his head far left in order to see them. His cheek throbbed and his right eye was half blind from swelling and dried blood. He couldn't imagine how bad he must look.

"Someone's coming," Keely whispered.

He turned and watched a figure slowly descend the wooden stairs. Black leather boots with stiletto heels, charcoal chap pants, a heavily studded leather bustier underneath a fringed motorcycle jacket. It *was* Maggie.

"Hi, guys," she greeted them. "It's so funny to see you again."

Again just the sight of her made Michael suffocate with guilt. "Mag," he said as she strode into the room. "I'm so sorry."

She looked confused. "About what?"

"That you ended up here. I should have never let you go. I'm sorry."

"Don't be stupid!" she snapped. "It's always about

you, isn't it, Michael? Did you think I was wasting away without Super-Michael to look after me? Wake up, dummy. I'm here because I want to be here. Not because of anything you did."

Michael swallowed, struggling to make sense of her words. "Why in hell would you want to be here?"

She shrugged lazily. "It's not exactly perfect, but I'm totally taken care of. Plenty of food and my pick of clothes. And the Commander keeps me safer than you ever could. In fact, I've got it real good compared to a lot."

Maggie smacked her gum and stared down at her nails. They had been painted a deep sparkly blue. A glittery powder shone on her eyelids, and her lips were a glossy plum shade. Outlandish, but she seemed okay with that. In fact, Maggie seemed into this whole charade.

"So, what about you? What have you been doing?" Maggie asked. Michael was amazed at her light, casual tone, as if they were old friends who'd bumped into each other on a busy street. "Did you ever find that whatchamacallit place? Nuvo Mudman?"

Michael opened his mouth, couldn't even respond, then finally took a deep breath and spoke. "Yeah," he mumbled. "But it wasn't exactly perfect either."

"Oh, really?" Maggie sounded delighted to hear it. She strode across the room and sat down on an over-turned crate. "So anyway, I have good news. Chiefy— that's the Commander, he likes it when I call him Chiefy—he's made his decision. You"—she pointed a blue-tipped finger at Diego—"are going to be his official hunter."

"Screw that!" Diego spat. "I'm not doing crap for those psychos!"

Maggie ignored him. "And you, Michael, will be made a slave." She smiled and clasped her hands. "Aren't you relieved?"

"That I'm a *slave?*" he hollered.

"Well, I mean, yeah. Hey, most people are put to death. You should be happy."

Michael stared at her in disbelief. She was even more loopy and damaged than before. And who could blame her, considering what she'd been through? It was his fault. Somehow he'd done this to her.

She smacked her gum and pivoted on her seat to face the girls.

"I'll be back for you three later," she told them. "After the feast I'm supposed to outfit you guys for the Commander."

"Outfit? What does that mean?" Liza demanded.

Maggie cocked her head. "Who are you?"

"Liza."

"Oh. I'm Maggie. I used to be Michael's girlfriend." She lifted her eyebrows. "Are you his new girlfriend?"

Liza didn't say anything. Maggie glanced from Liza to Michael and back again.

"Right. Anyway, Lisa, I'm supposed to make you and the other girls more, you know, presentable for the Commander. I've got some cool clothes and I can tell you what to do."

Liza, Irene, and Keely exchanged baffled, terrified glances.

"Don't worry," Maggie said in a sisterly sort of tone. "The important thing to remember is not to cry and to keep things lively. If they find you boring or uncooperative, you get thrown in the pits. So keep them interested."

"I think I'm going to be sick again," Liza mumbled.

"Oh no," Maggie said. "You definitely can't do that when you're with the men."

"Stop!" Michael shouted. An intense pain rattled through his head. It felt like his mind was kicking and screaming, refusing to accept what was happening. "Don't do this, Maggie. You've got to help us. See if you can get us out of here!"

Maggie slowly turned to face him, her face stony. "Don't tell me what to do!" she snapped. "You aren't the boss of me anymore! In fact"—she stood and smiled wickedly—"*I'm* the one in charge now."

THIRTY-FOUR

"WE'RE GOING TO CHECK EVERY BUILDING, EVERY CELLAR, AND every doghouse," Captain Tabori barked. "I want every inch of this town searched for clues."

"Yes, Captain," Jonah said as he quickly changed socks on the grimy floor of the old general store they were using as a headquarters.

It had taken them forever to find a way around the avalanche, and even when they had, they'd never picked up the trail again. Although he wouldn't say it aloud, Jonah knew that River had also given up, but the captain seemed determined to press on.

Then late that afternoon they'd come into Jasper Springs, a small rural village. They had found faint foot-prints leading to it. It was only one set, and the trail was old, judging by how frozen the prints were. But Tabori wanted the entire place scoured for any signs that the deserters might have come that way—as well as any useful supplies.

Like new socks. *Ahhh.* Jonah smiled as he slid his feet into a new pair of athletic crews. He would never take dry socks for granted again.

Suddenly the door clanged open and a small old man scrambled in, pushed by River's boot. A survivalist, probably. Everything about him was brown. Brown skin, tattered brown clothes, rheumy brown eyes, and filthy hair.

"Let me go!" he shouted in a raspy voice. Jonah noticed that even his teeth were brown.

"Captain!" River called. "I found this guy down on the trail. I think he knows something."

The captain's eyes widened. She quickly crossed the room and stood in front of the old man. "What did you see?" she demanded. "Tell me what you know, or I'll have these guys beat it out of you."

"I don't know nothin'!" the man yelped. "All I says is that some young people was in a back of a truck, then they pull me in here!"

The captain loomed closer until she was only an inch or so away from his face. "What truck? What kind of truck were they driving?"

The man stared back at her as if she were nuts. "They wasn't driving! They was with those crazy folks. The ones with the lines on their faces." He ran his index finger diagonally across his cheek.

"The Slash?" the captain asked, pulling back. Her typically pale face seemed to blanch even more.

"Yep. Them's the ones," the man said, nodding.

Captain Tabori's eyes darted around the room, as if searching for some sort of alternate reality. Then she screwed up her face and turned away. "Crap!" she shouted, kicking over a large sign that read, FRESH BAIT! CHECK OUT OUR LIVE NIGHT CRAWLERS! A second later she whirled back around as if remembering something. "The captives, were there five of them?" she asked.

"Think so. Couple a guys an' about three girls."

The captain's eyes squeezed shut and she stomped away. "Damn it."

A creeping numbness swept over Jonah's scalp and down his back. *The Slash? No. Please, no.* He thought of Atom and Mickey, the nice couple who'd helped him get through Missouri, and the horrible stories they'd told him about the Slash before they themselves were captured.

"When was this?" Jonah asked the old man. Maybe it wasn't too late. Maybe they could somehow find them and rescue them.

"Saw them drive past this morning," the man replied. "They your folks? 'Cause if they is, they sure done for now."

"No," Jonah muttered, thinking of his friends' faces. An image of Irene froze in his mind. It was over.

The old man nodded. "Yep. They dead. Once folks get taken by them, they don't never come back."

THIRTY-FIVE

DAMN! DIEGO HATED THIS FEELING OF HELPLESSNESS. HE
struggled one more time against the chains that bound
him against the wall, but it was useless.

Without the familiarity of the woods or the security
of the bow, he was just a guy with a bad leg and an even
worse attitude. But he refused to give up or play along
and hope for the best like the others. As long as he had
breath in him, he would put up a fight.

He remembered how Nonnie used to make him
promise that if anyone tried to put her in a nursing
home, he would kill her. Uncle Gilbert and the others
would shake their heads and chuckle, calling her a
spunky old broad. But Diego always knew she was
serious. Nonnie had always said, the day she had to

live by somebody else's rules would be the day she died.

He felt exactly the same way.

Irene let out a tiny whimper in her sleep and her head flopped toward him. The others also slept fitfully in their strange, half-strung-up positions. But Diego was too angry to even consider drifting off. Just the thought of one of those ugly brutes pawing at Irene and his body would simmer with rage, powering up his aching limbs.

One thing was sure, there was no way in hell he was going to help feed those assholes. He'd rather die. Even death by alligator would be better than a life of torture in this place.

A distant noise made him start. He looked up and saw Maggie coming down the stairs, rattling a ring of keys in her hand. An AK-47 was slung over her shoulder. As she reached the bottom step, she tripped in her high-heeled boots and stumbled into a crate. Everyone else woke with a start.

"Oops-a-daisy," she said with a slight giggle.

Irene stiffened against the wall. Diego knew what she was thinking. The feasting and merriment must be over and Maggie was coming for the girls. Just thinking about the Jabba the Hut commander having his way with Irene—or Keely or Liza—made his insides churn.

One by one she walked up and released the girls from their restraints. First Keely, followed by Irene and Liza. Next she trotted over to Michael and unlocked his shackles.

"What's going on?" he asked.

"I'm letting you out," she said. "Duh!"

Michael massaged his wrists and shot Diego a baffled expression. Diego gritted his teeth. So they were going too, huh? Why? To provide some sort of sick entertainment for those leather-clad creeps? To be an audience for whatever twisted things they put the girls through? No thanks.

As soon as Maggie unshackled him, he lunged forward for the rifle. Unfortunately, his arms were stiff and barely cooperative, and he ended up grabbing air instead.

"Hey, what are you trying to do?" Maggie said, stepping backward. She fumbled with her gun and pointed it at his chest. "Get back. I mean it."

"Or you'll what?" he asked, laughing ironically. "Shoot me? Go ahead!"

"Diego, stop it!" Irene shouted.

Michael scrambled over and grabbed him by the shoulders, holding him back. "What's wrong with you? You're going to get yourself killed!"

"I don't care!" Diego cried. He pushed Michael away and stepped up to Maggie. "Just shoot me! I dare you!" He couldn't take this place any longer. No matter what, it had to end now.

Maggie let out a frustrated sigh. "You need to calm down, dude," she said, waggling the gun in front of him like a scolding index finger. "I just got rid of the guard outside and now your yelling will bring more. And *then* how am I going to rescue you guys?"

THIRTY-SIX

THE ZOO WAS EERILY QUIET. IT MADE KEELY NERVOUS. SHE and the others meandered between the pens and cages in their lopsided line, a long rope tying each of them by their hands. Diego had made most of the knots himself, making them look tight when actually simply pulling their wrists apart would widen the rope enough for a quick escape. So far, though, that didn't seem to be necessary.

As they quietly made their way in the dark, listening to the snorts and snores all around them, it was difficult to tell the animal sounds from the human ones. Just like Maggie had said, most of the Slash seemed to be gone, sleeping off the effects of too much alcohol. They crept past a couple of them facedown on benches or stretched out on the cobbled paths. The few who were stirring were visibly drunk. Most staggered right past them, completely oblivious; one shouted unintelligible phrases but didn't seem capable of standing.

Keely glanced over at Maggie, who was striding along beside them, pretending to keep her rifle pointed at their heads. Or *was* she pretending? Keely couldn't quite buy her sudden change of mind yet. Maggie just didn't strike her as someone who'd do this out of the goodness of her leather-clad heart.

The path curved, leading them back into the wide courtyard. Keely recognized the low wall and roofed ticket booths of the front entrance. They were almost out.

Suddenly a monstrous shape emerged from the nearby trees. "Halt," it called. As it lumbered forward into the starlight, Keely could see a burly man in a red flame skullcap sitting atop a weary-looking donkey. He stopped beside Maggie and squinted down at her. "Your Highness?" he said in a slurred voice. "What are you doing out here?"

Maggie tossed her hair over her shoulder and giggled. "Oh, you know. The Commander wants me to outfit the prisoners for him, but it's so dark and I keep getting lost."

The man looked out over their ragtag little group, his gaze traveling up and down each girl's body. "Shit," he said, drawling out the word so that it sounded less like a complaint than a mating call. "This one taken yet?" He reached forward and grabbed Irene by the hair, pulling her—and as a result the rest of them—closer to him.

In front of her, Keely could see Diego stiffen.

"Yeah," Maggie replied matter-of-factly. "She's going to one of the men who found her."

"Too bad." The man let go of Irene and clopped down a ways to Keely, grabbing her chin with his rough, ungloved hand. "What about her?" he asked, his foul breath wafting over her.

"Sorry. They're all claimed," Maggie said, as if she were some sort of retailer who'd just run out of inventory.

"Huh," the man grumbled, noticeably put out. He turned toward Diego. "Would the Commander mind if I use this one for target practice?" He pulled a revolver out of his gun belt and pointed it unsteadily at Diego, cackling all the while.

Diego's face hardened and his hands clenched into tight fists. *Just keep cool,* Keely urged silently.

"Better not," Maggie said. "This guy is the Commander's new hunter. If you hurt him, he'll throw you in the pit for sure."

The man muttered a few curse words and then clumsily reholstered his gun.

"Sorry you had to miss some of the fun tonight," Maggie cooed, jutting out her lower lip in a gesture of pity. She lifted a bottle out of his saddle pack and took a long swig of murky liquid. A small trickle ran down the sides of her mouth and she wiped it up with her fingers in a rather overstated, sexy gesture. "I'm surprised you got the home brew," she said, handing the bottle back to him. "You know, there's still some looted bourbon back at the hall."

"Yeah?" he asked. Maggie nodded. "All *right!*" The man spurred the donkey with his engineer boots and they went clomping off into the distance.

"Okay, come this way," Maggie said after the sound died away. She led them past the ticket booths and down the gravel path to the parking lot. Once there, she slowly paced the lines of vehicles, scrutinizing them with her finger against her chin.

"That one," Keely said, pointing to the truck they'd arrived in. "I know it still has gas in it."

Maggie wrinkled up her face. "No, I hate trucks. It's such a rough ride."

"It's not like we have time to be choosy!" Diego snapped.

Maggie glared at him. "Hyper down. I know what I want." She sashayed past him toward a tarp-draped vehicle and pulled back the cover. Underneath was a gold PT Cruiser. "This one."

"But we won't all fit," Irene pointed out.

"Sure, you will," Maggie replied. "I don't care what you guys say. This is the one we're taking."

"Fine, let's just hurry," Michael said, pulling his hands out of the rope knot. Everyone else did the same.

As they reached for the back door, Maggie stopped them. "No. Only Diego rides in front. Everyone else lies down in the back."

"What?" Keely exclaimed. "We'll be squashed."

Maggie's pouty expression returned. "Listen, I've

been wanting to ride in this car for a long time now. This is the one we're taking and that's final."

"Okay, okay." Michael held up his hands in a surrender gesture. "Let's just do what she says."

Maggie popped open the back door and Irene, Michael, Liza, and Keely climbed inside. Each of them stretched out as best as they could, having to squeeze right up against the person next to them. Keely ended up pushed into Liza, her face in her hair, her legs tangled up with hers.

"Watch your fingers," Maggie said in a singsongy voice. Then she slammed down the rear door, enveloping them in darkness.

Keely felt the car jostle as Diego and Maggie sat in the front seat. A second later the engine started.

"Michael," Keely whispered. "Why is she doing this?"

"I don't know," he replied.

"I don't like this," Liza said, whimpering slightly. "I don't like *her.*"

"We've just got to trust her," Keely said.

"You guys, *shhh!*" Irene gasped. "We're stopping."

Sure enough, the car was rolling to a complete halt. Keely could hear Maggie flirting and sweet-talking.

"Could you open the gate, please?" she asked.

"Where're you going?" asked a gravelly male voice.

"I'm taking the Commander's new hunter out to catch us some food," Maggie replied. "He needs to prove himself or be put to death."

There was a pause, followed by crunching footsteps. "Your car is riding really low in the back," said the man's voice, sounding closer.

Liza let out a muffled sob.

"*Shhh*. Keep still and quiet," Michael said in the barest of whispers.

The footsteps crept even closer. "Open the rear door and I'll take a look for you," the man said. He sounded only inches away.

Liza's breathing grew faster and faster, rocking Keely against the metal frame. The girl was clearly losing it.

Suddenly there came a rattling sound, like someone fiddling with the latch outside.

Liza took a deep breath. Acting on instinct, Keely clamped her hand over her mouth before the scream could escape. Liza struggled against her. Fearing she might shake the car, Keely held her down tightly with her arms and legs, pressing her up against Michael's back.

"That's just the hunting equipment," came Maggie's voice. The rattling stopped. "Now open the gate, pretty please?" she continued. "The Commander is going to be really, really mad at you if we're late."

The footsteps hurried away. A few seconds later Keely heard a metal clang and the car accelerated again. She released her grip on Liza and let go of her mouth.

Liza gasped frantically. "I couldn't breathe! What were you trying to do? Kill me?"

"I'm sorry," Keely said. "I was just trying to keep you quiet so we wouldn't get caught."

"You were trying to hurt me!"

"Liza," Michael said, groping backward for her. "You were freaking. Keely was only trying to save us."

"Whose side are you on?" Liza screamed.

"No one's. I mean . . ." Michael sighed loudly. "Everyone's."

"I hate this," Liza said, sobbing. "I hate everything."

Keely felt an intense rush of sympathy. She understood Liza's pain completely—stuck in a nightmare world where no one behaved the way you needed them to.

"Everybody stop and listen!" Irene cried suddenly.

They all paused, straining for any noise. "I don't hear anything," Keely said.

"That's just it," Irene replied. "I think maybe . . . we're safe?"

THIRTY-SEVEN

As the car slowed to a stop, Liza's heartbeat accelerated. She had no idea how long they'd been cooped up in a tangled heap in the back of that sardine can, but it seemed like hours. The smell of the dirty car floor mixed with body odor was making her feel nauseous, and she had been praying for it to come to an end. But now that they were stopping, her discomfort gave way to panic.

The hatch opened and Liza was surprised to see the light of morning haloing Maggie's blond hair.

"Okay. Get out," she said.

They climbed from the car and stretched their cramped limbs, staring up and down the empty highway.

"There's no one after us yet," Maggie said, noticing their wariness. "You're safe."

"I don't understand," Michael said, walking up to her. "Why did you save us?"

A sly smile crept across her face. "That's right. *I* saved you. I want you to always remember that it was me, stupid Maggie. You had nothing to do with it."

He shook his head in amazement. "I really appreciate it. Seriously. And I promise I'll make it up to you."

"Uh-uh," she said. "Now we're square. You helped me out, now I'm helping you. We don't owe each other anything after this."

A loud honking noise sounded in the distance.

"What was that?" Liza asked.

"It's the Slash alarm," Maggie replied. "They know you're gone."

"We've got to go," Keely said, heading for the Cruiser's driver's side. "Everyone get in the car."

"No way." Maggie shook her head. "I found my home. I'm staying."

"What?" Liza was stunned. "How can you call that hellhole a home? Those guys are animals!"

Maggie put her hands on her hips. "You think I want to be one of you peons, having to scrounge for everything you need? No, thank you. Here I'm a *queen.*" She flourished her arms in a grand gesture. "I've got a hundred men taking care of me. And I get whatever I need—for free."

Not for free, Liza thought, looking at Maggie with a mixture of pity and disgust. The poor girl thought she had it so good, she couldn't see those savages were just using her.

"Come on, Maggie," Michael said. "You've got to come with us!"

"Don't tell me what to do!" she shouted.

"Hurry, guys," Keely called. "We have to leave, now!"

"Maggie, please," Michael pleaded. "You don't know what's good for you."

"Who says? You? What do you know?"

"Michael! Let's go!" Diego urged.

"I can't just leave her here! When they find out she helped us, they'll hurt her!"

"I can take care of myself!" Maggie snapped.

"Fine. I know what to do," Diego said. He stalked toward Maggie, cocked his fist, and punched her in the jaw. Maggie crumpled to the ground.

"Oh my God!" Irene screamed. "Diego! Stop!"

Liza watched Irene's face, feeling her horror. Irene's worst nightmare was finally happening: Diego was losing his mind.

Michael rushed over and grabbed Diego, pulling him backward. "What's wrong with you?" he shouted. "Are you insane?"

"I'm trying to help her!" Diego cried, pushing Michael off him.

"How? By beating her up?"

Diego held out his arms. "You said it yourself. She doesn't know what's good for her. Now it will look like we *forced* her to help us. Maybe now they won't be so upset with her!"

Michael stared at him, speechless. Liza also felt stunned. It was horrible. But in a way, it did make sense. If Maggie refused to go with them, maybe this really was the only way to help her.

"See, Michael? You don't always know what's right," Maggie said, struggling to a sitting position, her left hand clamped against her cheek. "You think you can take care of me, but you can't. You couldn't even stop this."

Michael gaped at her, his expression equal parts guilt and disgust. In the distance the horn continued to blare.

"Guys, come on!" Keely shouted, revving the engine. Irene scrambled into the car. Liza followed.

"Let's go, Michael," Diego said. But Michael continued to stare at Maggie, as if in a daze. Diego placed his hand on Michael's chest and started pushing him toward the Cruiser.

"What's the matter, Michael? Want to take a swing at me too?" Maggie burst out laughing, blood gushing from her mouth.

Liza shuddered. She hadn't realized how far gone Maggie was until now. Michael finally came to his senses and jumped inside the car with Diego. As Keely sped away, Liza turned and stared at Maggie's shrinking form. She was still holding herself and laughing.

You poor, broken, stupid thing, Liza thought. *How the hell did you get so fried?*

THIRTY-EIGHT

STEP, *OW!* STEP, *OW!*

Amber waddled toward the auditorium, her swollen ankles protesting with every footfall. It felt strange to walk this far after so much bed rest, and she wasn't sure if she should be doing it at all. But when the notice came that there would be a mandatory meeting for everyone in Novo Mundum's main lecture hall, it didn't say everyone except bedridden pregnant people.

Besides, it was nice to be out of that stuffy room for a change.

She already had a good idea what the meeting was about. It was common knowledge that Jonah and the rest of the search party had returned yesterday without any of the deserters. She smiled just thinking about it.

Knowing her friends had gotten away with her help made her feel better than she had in a long time. And she couldn't wait to hear Dr. Slattery's take on the whole thing.

"Good afternoon," a few people greeted her as she dragged herself up the building's concrete steps. She smiled back at them, too winded to reply.

The crowd parted for her as she plodded into the lecture hall, everyone smiling and gesturing to empty seats. Amber was beginning to feel like the Novo Mundum mascot. Or court jester. All she had to do to interest them was shuffle past, her big belly leading the way.

She settled herself in a seat at the end of an aisle, close to a door she knew led to some bathrooms. Stretching out her legs, she put her puffy, aching feet on the armrests in front of her and leaned back to catch her breath.

Dr. Slattery strode onto the stage and tapped on the center podium's microphone. "May I have your attention, please?" he said. Amber was surprised at how crumpled and decrepit he looked. His face was as creased as his white doctor's coat, and small clumps of his hair stuck up at odd angles. "As you might know," he began, "five of our very own left Novo Mundum eight days ago."

No shit, Amber thought. An expectant murmur welled up in the crowd.

Dr. Slattery took a breath and continued. "Unfortunately, a couple of these people had been caught breaking our rules, and instead of working things out with us, they decided to leave. This was a rash, foolhardy, and unnecessary action. We are reasonable people here. We are not like President MacCauley's so-called government."

Amber narrowed her eyes at him. *Right,* she said inwardly. *We're worse.*

"I was immensely saddened to learn that two of the escapees were my only daughter, Liza, whom I love more than anything, and Michael Bishop, whom I had truly respected and admired. I blame myself for having trusted Michael, not realizing that he was spinning a web of lies and turning the others against me—including my young, impressionable daughter. I will never forgive myself for that." Dr. Slattery paused, as if overcome with emotion.

Boo frigging hoo, Amber thought. She glanced around at the crowd. Everyone was gazing at him sympathetically. She found Jonah sitting near the front, slouched in his chair, his eyes fixed on the wall as if not really seeing it. "Traitor," she muttered under her breath. A few rows behind him sat Irene's father and brother, looking just as dazed. She wondered how they must be feeling.

"I should have seen it," Dr. Slattery resumed. "I had no idea of the distrust Michael was instilling in my daughter and the rest of them until it was too late. By the time I reached out, they had already escaped into the dangers of the Big Empty, where they were taken by the Slash and most likely killed." His voice tapered off as a loud gasp welled up among the crowd.

What? Amber felt like she'd been stabbed in the heart. *Did he say killed? No. This has to be a trick.* She looked around the audience, hoping she might have simply misunderstood, but their stricken expressions told her otherwise.

Her eyes fell on Mr. Margolis and Aaron. They looked so pale and broken. Seeing them made it suddenly feel real. Her friends were gone. Irene . . . Michael . . . Diego . . . *Keely!* They were dead. *At the hands of the Slash!* She couldn't think of anything more horrible.

Frank stood up from the front row, mounted the stage, and helped Dr. Slattery to a nearby chair. The two brothers were the very picture of anguish, yet Amber couldn't quite buy it. They were still lying about why her friends left. They might be truly upset about Liza, but the whole meeting was still a subtle "this is what will happen to you if you try to leave" type speech.

Frank returned to the microphone and worked his jaw before finally speaking. "I'm not very good at these things, but . . . uh . . ." He swallowed hard and tugged at his collar. "Could you all please join us in a moment of silence for our fallen?"

A hush fell over the hall as everyone bowed their heads. Meanwhile Amber glanced around the room, her eyes cloudy with tears. Traitors. Liars. Evil slime. Blind, stupid sheep! She hated them all. The Slash might have actually committed the murders, but these people were the ones who'd killed her friends—through ignorance or treachery.

Amber grasped tightly to her anger, nursing it large and healthy until it overshadowed her grief.

"Thank you," Frank said after a minute or two. "Now, there is one more item of business, some news that can hopefully offer some comfort in the midst of our loss. My brother, as you all know, has been hard at work developing vaccines for potential new strains of the virus that changed our world. I'm pleased to announce that he has finally cultivated a vaccine that shows great promise. In this time of mourning those who are gone, I'd like us to focus on protecting ourselves and each other as we move forward. We will begin injecting Mundians with the vaccine shortly, and we're happy to answer your questions as they arise. And now the meeting is adjourned."

Everyone seemed reluctant to leave. Some people still sat quietly in their chairs; others chatted in hushed yet eager tones with their neighbors. Amber felt chills pass through her as she tried to process one horror after another. Her friends, gone. And now this . . . a *vaccine?* Against the very Strain 8 virus Dr. Slattery himself was creating? No way, something seriously messed up was going on. What the hell did the bastard really intend to inject them all with?

Out of the corner of her eye Amber saw Jonah rise from his seat and amble toward the nearest exit. Summoning her strength, she pushed herself onto her feet and followed him, veering clumsily around a few standing stragglers. Again her ankles throbbed, but Amber barely felt it. Sheer rage seemed to be fueling her limbs.

"Jonah!" she called as she caught up with him on the outside steps.

He turned and waited for her.

"Amber," he said in an empty voice, as if he were identifying her instead of greeting her.

"You happy now?" she seethed. "This place you love so much drove our friends to their death!"

Jonah looked past her, his face void of emotion. "They brought it on themselves."

"How can you say that!" she hissed. "Don't you even care about what happened to them at all?"

"They made a mistake," he said, robot-like. "They shouldn't have left."

"Shut up, traitor! All you care about is yourself!" Amber shouted. It felt good to release the rage. But the fact that Jonah just stood there and accepted it without much resistance took a bit of the thrill away.

"They shouldn't have left," he repeated. Amber wondered if he was trying to convince himself as well.

By now the anger was almost spent, and she knew tears would be close behind. Taking a deep breath, Amber leaned forward and hurled her last jab. "I hope you have nightmares about this, you son of a bitch," she muttered. "And from now on, I never want to talk to you again."

She whirled around and tried to stomp down the concrete steps but ended up falling backward instead. Jonah caught her before she could smack against the concrete.

"Let go of me!" she cried, struggling out of his grasp. More tentatively, she again tried to head down the stairs.

"Let me help you, kiddo."

Amber lifted her head and saw Dr. MacTavish descending the steps toward her. She looked her usual grumpy self, yet Amber found she was happy to see her. Grabbing Amber's arm with both of her hands, the doctor gently supported her down the rest of the stairs.

"Thanks," Amber said once they reached the sidewalk.

"Sure thing," the doctor said. "Now listen," she added, lowering her voice, "you need to be careful. I mean it. You have to take it easy—and I don't just mean physically." She gave Amber a quick wink, did a swift about-face, and strode away.

Amber watched her go. She still felt smashed after the horrible news of her friends and terrified of what Dr. Slattery's "vaccine" was really about, but amid the wreckage and fear she sensed a tiny flicker of light. At least she wasn't totally, completely alone here.

THIRTY-NINE

DIEGO SAT SLUMPED IN A DUSTY CORNER OF THE TRAIN CAR, pretending to rest. The rhythmic rocking did give the illusion of being in a giant cradle, but he was way too tense to drift off. A plan was forming in his mind, and he needed the time and space to work out the details.

Thankfully the others seemed to be avoiding him. The car they'd hopped the morning before had ended up being full of loot scavenged, he imagined, from towns and cities in the Big Empty. The others had searched the assorted crates, uncovering a couple of cans of beans, clean blankets, and even some medical supplies. Irene set right to work swabbing and bandaging Michael's face while Keely opened the beans and passed them around.

Diego felt superfluous. He missed his bow and arrows

and the familiarity of the forest. Now they were heading toward some unknown city where they would face soldiers, cold buildings, and lines and lines of people— his definition of hell. Once again he could feel himself giving up control of his life. And he wanted it to stop.

Which was why he'd come up with the plan.

It was clear the group didn't need him anymore—or trust him, probably. Even though he'd been fantasizing about hitting someone for a long while, it had given him no pleasure to hit Maggie. In fact, it repulsed him just thinking about it. And Irene's nervous stares only made it worse. So, he figured, why torment them any longer? As soon as he got the chance, he'd slip away and head for the nearest thatch of wilderness.

"Diego?"

He glanced up automatically at the sound of Irene's voice.

She lifted one of the cans of Ranch Beans. "There's some more food left. You want it?" She sounded casual, but her eyes still looked cautious.

He shook his head. "No thanks."

"Okay."

They stared at each other for a long awkward moment before he finally looked away. It killed him how detached they'd become. He'd been so focused on leading them all to safety, and there had still ended up being one major casualty—his special connection with Irene was gone for good. Now there was no reason to stay.

He shifted positions to ease the pressure on his leg.

Over the steady clack of the train he could hear the others talking, trying to predict the direction of the train they'd hopped.

"I think we're headed west," Keely said.

"No, east," said Irene. "Maybe northeast."

We're going south, Diego said to himself. He could tell by the gradual change in temperature and the angle of the sun streaming through cracks in the roof. But he wasn't going to share those facts aloud.

Wherever they ended up, he wouldn't be staying long.

FORTY

MICHAEL TOOK A DEEP BREATH, WARMING TO THE PROSPECT OF being back in the occupied territory. He'd always operated better in civilization, though after days of travel on the train no one was sure exactly what civilization they'd landed in.

Diego leaned his head out of the gap in the rail yard fence. "It's all clear," he whispered. "Come on."

Michael shimmied under the bowed chain link, emerging onto a tree-lined street in the heart of . . . somewhere. The climate was warm—maybe low to mid-seventies—and the air was thick and soupy. They each shed their jackets and glanced around at the scanty mid-morning foot traffic.

"Wherever we are, it sure is big," Diego observed,

glancing at the glass-and-steel skyscrapers looming off to their left.

Michael inhaled deeply, enjoying the grimy scent of the city. He'd missed this. The tall buildings and wide sidewalks and brisk tempo of life. This was where he belonged.

Of course, there was still the lingering threat that he could be stopped and questioned and identified as a fugitive. But that was the only good thing about getting slashed on the cheek. At least he didn't resemble his old self as much with a big gauze bandage taped over half his face. Then again, it also made him stick out.

"We should keep walking," Diego said, "find out where we are."

They ambled down the road until they came to a wide intersection. All around them stood brown brick buildings with shuttered windows and dusty, deserted storefronts. On the side of a derelict bus stop hung a large, faded poster of an astronaut hovering sideways with planet Earth looming behind him. Visit the NASA Space Museum, it said in big block letters. Over it in bright green script someone had spray-painted, *Grounded for Life.*

"I think we're in Houston," Keely said. She pointed to the remains of a flyer plastered on a nearby telephone pole advertising a livestock show at the Astrodome. The dates were for the fall of 2002.

"Houston? My aunt Marie lives here!" Irene exclaimed. "I used to come here all the time to visit her.

But it seems so different now. Less noisy and smoggy."

"Is your aunt still alive?" Michael asked.

"I hope so. She was six months ago. We told the authorities that was where we were headed when we evacuated."

"Then we should get in touch with her. We could use her place as our new base." He paused. "Don't you think?"

Everyone glanced at Diego.

He held up his hands. "Whatever. Sounds good to me."

"Let's do it, then," Michael said, nodding. "Where does she live?"

"The Heights, not far from downtown," Irene replied. She glanced up at the tallest buildings to orient herself and pointed down to their right. "That way. Jefferson should lead us to Washington Avenue, which will take us right to her place."

They started down the street. Michael rolled up his sleeves as he walked. Considering it was December, he couldn't believe how warm it was. It seemed impossible that only a few days before, he'd been dealing with snow and ice and frostbite.

"Oh, I can't wait," Irene said happily. "It will be so good to see family."

"And get a shower," Liza added.

"And a good night's sleep," Keely chimed in.

"You five! Stop right there and turn around! Hands where I can see them!"

Oh no! Michael's blood froze in his veins. He raised

his arms and slowly pivoted about. The others did the same. Behind them, a soldier stood frowning down the barrel of his rifle as he pointed it directly at their heads.

"Oh my God," Liza gasped.

The man stepped closer and looked them up and down. He stopped at Liza. "How old are you?" he barked. "Why aren't you in school?"

"I—I —" Liza stammered, her body trembling.

Michael took a good look at the soldier. He was older than most, maybe late forties, with gray streaks in the sides of his close-cropped hair. On his left hand shone a wide gold wedding band.

A family man—probably a cop in his former life, Michael thought, instinctively sizing him up. *Married twenty years before widowed. Maybe two or three kids.*

Suddenly he had an idea.

"Please, sir," he said, leaning between Liza and the soldier. "I can explain everything."

The man turned his attention to Michael. "Well?"

"My girlfriend and I"—he threw his arm around Liza's shaking shoulders—"we're getting married today. And we invited our best friends to witness. It's true she had to miss school. But that was only because her father's against it. She's going to go right back tomorrow."

"You know you are not supposed to leave school grounds without proper authorization," the soldier said. He was still frowning, but Michael was heartened to hear most of the sternness had left his voice.

Michael sighed guiltily. "I'm very sorry, sir. We just thought . . . you know, in these crazy times . . . that love was more important than ever." He pulled Liza to him in a sideways hug.

The soldier continued to scowl at them. "What happened to your face?" he asked, gesturing toward Michael's cheek with the end of his rifle.

"Her cat clawed me while I was trying to help it down from a branch," Michael said. He was amazed at how quickly the lies tumbled out of him, almost of their own accord. "Want to see?" he added, gripping one end of the tape. "The doctor said to keep it under wraps while it's still oozing, but I could show you if you like."

The man instinctively jerked backward. "No, no. That won't be necessary."

"Yeah, I won't be doing that again." Michael kissed the top of Liza's head. "I love you, babe, but next time your cat finds its own way down, okay?"

"Okay," she said with a nervous laugh.

For a long moment the soldier just looked at them. Then slowly he lowered his weapon. "All right," he said. "I'll let you off this time."

"Thank you, sir," Michael said, breathing deeply for the first time in minutes. "I really appreciate it."

The man broke into a small smile. "I remember what it's like," he said wistfully. "But no loitering, okay? And you ought not to travel in a pack. Makes people nervous."

"Right," Michael said nodding. "We won't. Thank you, sir."

"On your way, then. And congratulations. I wish you all the luck in the world."

"Thanks," Michael said, hurrying down the block with the others.

We'll need it.

FORTY-ONE

"THIS IS IT," IRENE SAID, STOPPING IN FRONT OF APARTMENT 4-D. An ornate, silver mezuzah shone on the door frame and a tiny placard above the doorbell read M. Margolis. Aunt Marie's place. Just as she remembered it.

She tried the buzzer and found it was broken, so she raised her hand and knocked.

A moment later she knocked again.

Irene turned and looked at the others. "Maybe she's napping," she said.

They waited another minute.

"She might not be home," Keely said.

"Do you think she'd mind if we broke in?" Diego asked. "I mean, it is an emergency."

Irene frowned. "No. Probably not." Instinctively she

reached down and turned the knob. The door opened. "It's unlocked," she said in surprise.

One by one they shuffled into the dim apartment.

"Aunt Marie?" Irene called. But there was no answer.

She pushed open the drapes hanging over the large glass balcony door and a cloud of dust swirled over her, making her cough.

"Um . . . Irene?" Keely said tentatively. "It doesn't seem like anyone lives here."

Someone hit a light switch. "Electricity's on," Michael said. He walked into the kitchen nook and turned a knob on the faucet. Brown water sputtered noisily from the spigot. "Water too. Although it hasn't been running through the pipes for a while."

"Look here," Diego said, pointing to an upturned wooden stand with a long, frayed cable draped over it. "I think someone grabbed the TV set."

A shaky feeling came over Irene as she noticed the thick layer of dust on the furniture and the wisps of cobwebs hanging in every corner. Over Michael's shoulder she could see the pantry doors hanging open in the kitchen, its shelves empty.

"Maybe she went on a trip?" she mumbled. She knew it was a lame thing to say, but she had to anyway. She'd been so looking forward to being with family. Assuming the worst would only tear her up even more.

Keely walked up beside her. "Maybe she did," she offered. "You think she'd mind if we stayed here anyway? Maybe helped ourselves to a few of her things?"

"No," Irene replied, smiling gratefully at Keely. "She wouldn't mind."

For the next several minutes they rummaged through drawers and cabinets. Liza found a package of noodles in a far corner of the pantry and Keely uncovered a stack of food coupons in a wooden box on the bookshelf.

"I'll boil us some drinking water," Keely said, pulling a saucepan out of a cabinet.

"I'm going to try and find some batteries for this radio," Michael said, holding up a black boom box. "Maybe we can get some information."

"Can I be first in the shower?" Liza asked.

"Go ahead," Irene said, gesturing toward the bathroom. "I'm going to poke about some more. Aunt Marie's notorious for hiding things."

She wandered into the main bedroom and turned on the light. It was just as she remembered except for the open, empty jewelry box. On the bed was the gingham quilt she remembered Aunt Marie making with her mother. Irene smiled sadly, tracing its intricate stitching with her forefinger. Her aunt had made another one for Irene's bat mitzvah, the exact same pattern, only with reds and golds instead of blues. Irene had wanted so badly to take it with them to Novo Mundum, but her father had talked her out of it, saying it was too heavy.

Opening up the closet, Irene suddenly caught a whiff of her aunt's perfume, lingering on the clothes and coats. *White something,* she thought, trying to remember the name. She ran her hands over the soft, fleecy material, checking pockets and uncovering a couple more coupons.

As she made her way down toward the end of the row of clothes, she tripped over something on the floor of the closet. She bent down and pulled a cardboard hatbox into the light.

She always did have a thing for hats, Irene thought with a chuckle. Maybe she'd try it on—just for a laugh.

She set the box on the bed and sat down beside it. Lifting off the lid, Irene gasped to find a stash of old photographs inside. Some color, some black and white. She dug through them eagerly. There was one of her aunt at the school where she taught. There was Irene at age seven, dressed as a ballerina for Halloween. Another of Aaron on his tenth birthday, proudly holding up a new GameBoy.

Just then her fingers alighted on a bigger photo, buried deep in the box. She slowly unearthed it, watching as her parents' faces appeared smiling, followed by her and Aaron's toothy grins.

Our last family portrait, Irene thought, tears slipping down her cheeks. She slowly traced her finger over each frozen face. This was a treasure more valuable than a whole ream of food coupons.

Suddenly she couldn't pretend any longer that things were all right. Everything was scary and horrible and very, very wrong. Her father and brother were so far away. Her aunt was nowhere to be found. And her mother was gone forever. Just like the happy life she used to have with her family and just like the carefree Irene in the photos.

Holding the family portrait to her chest, Irene fell back against the quilt and let herself cry.

FORTY-TWO

DIEGO STOOD ON THE BALCONY OF THE FOURTH-FLOOR APARTMENT, looking out over the dank, crumbling city. For a place under military rule, it sure looked trashed. There were bits of paper and rusted cans everywhere. And every fanatic in the area seemed to have his or her own can of spray paint. *God Is Punishing Us!* seemed to be the common theme or, *Repent!* Then there was one glib comment sprayed along the side of an abandoned, wheelless bus: *Strain 7's World Tour!*

Why am I even here? Diego wondered, a fresh batch of helpless anger rising inside him. How could he, a country boy, be any help to them in the city? He couldn't. Especially if they thought he was mental.

So why not leave? Now was as good a time as any.

He should just walk out the door and never return.

Only . . . he had to see Irene. Just one last time.

Diego pushed away from the balcony and walked back inside, heading toward the bedroom Irene had gone into. He would tell her he was going out for some supplies or something. It was lame, but at least he'd get one final look at her face.

Reaching the bedroom, Diego flung open the door and immediately froze. Irene was lying on the bed, sobbing into a pillow. Scattered around her on the quilt was a mosaic of photographs. In one he recognized her smile on a curly-haired toddler sitting in the arms of a beautiful woman. *Pictures of her family.*

Diego's heart seemed to be struggling inside him. He had an overwhelming urge to go to her, yet part of him was afraid that it would only make things worse. He fumbled for the doorknob and the latch let out a loud clicking sound. Irene immediately sat up and turned toward him, her eyes wide.

"Oh . . . h-hey," she said, rubbing her eyes with the backs of her hands. "I was just . . . napping."

Diego felt a pang of guilt. She couldn't even trust him with her feelings.

And why should she? he wondered.

For days he'd been so busy being pissed at the world, and he'd wondered why she wouldn't join him in his outrage. Now he got why. She wasn't glossing over her anger—*he* was the one using anger to avoid what he really felt—the fear and uncertainty. And when he pushed all of that away, he pushed her along with it.

Slowly, as if in a trance, he shut the door behind him and walked over to the edge of the bed. He sat down beside her and cupped her tearstained face in his hands, looking deep into her eyes. "I'm sorry," he murmured. "I'm just . . . sorry."

Irene's mouth trembled and a new layer of wetness covered her eyes. Then all at once she threw her arms around him tightly, burrowing her face into his sweater. Diego closed his eyes, breathing in the familiar scent of her hair.

"It's okay," he said, stroking her back and rocking slightly.

As her sobs gradually subsided, he could feel his rage slowly evaporate. He'd been angry too long. He'd been running and hiding from things, forgetting the one thing that really mattered most—her. The city might feel wrong, but this felt right.

He couldn't leave now. Irene needed him. Besides, even if he tried, he wouldn't survive anyway.

Because he needed Irene too.

FORTY-THREE

Liza stood in the doorway to the bedroom, staring at the sight in front of her—Diego holding Irene. Irene was crying quietly and he was saying something in low, soothing tones.

She had gone in to look for some clean clothes after her shower and was surprised to find them like that. She'd thought they weren't really together anymore. And she'd even toyed with the idea that she and Diego might have a chance at something, with the way everything was unraveling between her and Michael.

Liza searched her feelings. Was she upset? *No.* For some reason, she wasn't. The two of them looked so . . . right. Like two puzzle pieces that come together to form a more complete picture. Besides, if she was going to be honest with herself, she wasn't really attracted to Diego that way. She'd just appreciated the way he accepted and understood her. Plus she'd admired his strength and leadership. He'd been the anti-Michael while Michael had been a lifeless shell.

She slowly backed away and shut the door before they could see her there. Turning around, she ran right into Keely, who stood in the hallway, towel-drying her hair. She was wearing a fresh set of clothes—a long skirt and slightly faded white blouse taken from the aunt's other bedroom.

"Hey, I'm going out to buy us some food," Keely said. "Want to come with me?"

"Where's Michael?"

"Sleeping on the couch."

Liza frowned. "Will it be safe?"

"Don't worry. It's after school hours. As long as we don't draw a lot of attention to ourselves, we'll be fine."

Liza thought for a moment. It would be nice to get out for a while and clear her mind. "Okay."

They finished dressing and headed out onto the street. Liza wore a small embroidered purse containing some of the food vouchers, and Keely carried a large cloth sack and an empty glass jug she'd carefully washed out.

As they turned onto a busy, shop-lined avenue, Liza folded her arms across her chest and hunched her shoulders. Until the moment they'd snuck out of the train yard, her only mental picture of life in the post–Strain 7 inhabited zones had come from what she could piece together from the horror stories told by Novo Mundum's recruits. It had sounded bad, but she'd never expected it to be this bad. Everything was worn and ugly and neglected. The buildings were covered with graffiti, and the cracked, muddy streets were full of debris.

For a few blocks it felt like she and Keely were in a stereotypical ghost town—no signs of life at all. Only clumps of paper blowing across the roads and the occasional tank perched ominously in the center of an intersection. Then they turned a corner and saw a long line of people trailing out of a voucher bank. It hurt to look at them. Everyone looked lost: their eyes sunken, their expressions hollow, as if all the joy had been leeched out of them. No one smiled and greeted them like in Novo Mundum. In fact, the people here barely looked at them at all.

Except for the soldiers.

As they approached the next crossroad, Liza could see an armed, helmeted guard glowering at them from the weed-choked median.

"Relax. Pretend you belong," Keely muttered out of the side of her mouth.

Liza let her arms swing at her sides and gazed up at the sky as if checking the weather. Soon they had completely passed him without incident.

"Good job," Keely whispered.

As they crossed the street, Liza turned and stared at Keely. She looked so pretty with her freshly washed hair pulled back in a clip. For so long Liza had been jealous of her, but not because she was beautiful. Instead it was another, deeper quality about Keely that made Liza feel inadequate. Her self-assuredness. Keely clearly knew how to take care of herself. Liza couldn't help but admire that about her. Michael too—which was why she'd been so jealous.

Liza bit her lip. A question that had been nagging at her pushed its way to the front of her mind.

"Keely? Can I ask you something?"

"Sure," she said.

"What's the story between Maggie and Michael?"

Keely pursed her lips. "I don't know everything," she said. "All I know is that Maggie used to be his girlfriend back in New York. When the virus hit, he stayed with her out of loyalty and tried to take care of her, even though his heart wasn't in it anymore. Then she got mixed up with a bad crowd and they ended up getting framed for stealing. Michael had to grab her and run."

"Has she always been . . . ?" Liza faltered, searching for the right word.

"A nut job?" Keely finished. "You can say it. Actually, I don't know. I feel bad for Michael giving up so much for her, but I also feel sorry for her." She paused and shook her head. "I don't know. Maybe it worked out for the best. Maggie never could have made it here. She's so dependent—always expecting men to take care of her. I guess in a way, she got just what she wanted."

Liza nodded absently, her mind reeling. Michael had accidentally called her Maggie that one time. Was that how he saw her? In a way, she'd always expected men to take care of her too. First Dad and Uncle Frank, then Michael—even Diego.

She remembered Maggie refusing to come with them, proudly calling herself a queen. And she, Liza, had always been referred to as Novo Mundum's princess. Maybe she'd been more like Maggie than she'd care to admit.

No more, she told herself. No matter how bad things got, she never wanted to end up like Maggie.

"There's a market," Keely said, gesturing toward a firehouse-red brick building with a tattered green awning. A handmade sign read, NEW SHIPMENTS! On another someone had scrawled, OUT OF POTATOES.

"Okay," Keely said, opening Liza's purse and pulling out the vouchers. "The yellow ones are worth ten points. The pink ones are worth five and the white ones are worth one point each. Each food item is assigned a point value. And remember, they don't like to make change, so save the yellow ones for really big things."

"Can you still pay with real money?"

Keely shrugged. "It depends. There were some places back home that still accepted it. But they were becoming more and more rare before I left."

Liza looked at her. There was a slight wistfulness in her tone as she talked about home. Keely never talked about her previous life, and it was surprising to think she might actually miss it.

"Let's get in and out as quick as we can," Keely

added, heading toward the door. "They get nervous if people dawdle."

"Okay." Liza took a deep breath and followed Keely inside.

The store was small and dimly lit by a couple of buzzing, flickering tube lights. A surly-looking man sat on a stool in a corner in front of a couple of plastic vats of liquid. An equally sour-faced woman stood behind the pay counter, glowering at the customers as they walked in.

Keely walked right up to the man. "How fresh is the milk?" she asked.

"Farmer brought it just this morning," he replied.

She handed him the bottle. "Can I fill this up, please?"

"Hang on, let me get the tap."

Keely turned and pressed the bag into Liza's arms. "This might take a while. Go ahead and gather the rest of the stuff," she said, gesturing toward the back of the store.

Liza glanced about. The proprietress was glaring right at her. "All right," she said, heading deeper into the store.

The shelves were mostly empty, and Liza was aghast at the condition of things. Cans without labels costing ten points each. A box of expired Fruit Roll-Ups costing twenty. The fresh produce was even more expensive. Fifteen points for a bunch of dirty, spindly carrots. Ten points for a head of cabbage.

Most of what the store had to offer were large bins of

government-issue protein bars, each wrapped in a plain brown label, costing one point apiece. Another tub held an assortment of protein shake packets for two points each. Liza shuddered at the flavors—cherry-banana cocktail, strawberry-vanilla swirl, lime pie surprise.

Okay, you can do this, she told herself. *Don't go crazy and spend everything. We don't know how long we'll be here.*

She set about filling her bag, counting up the total as she went. When she headed to the pay counter, she had fifteen protein bars, five shake packets, a bag of rice, a box of army surplus vitamins, and her one high-dollar item: a small first aid kit.

"That'll be forty points," the woman said.

"And the milk too," Liza said, pointing at Keely.

"Fifty even, then."

As Liza counted out the vouchers, the woman scowled at her. "You're new, aren't you?"

Liza felt a rush of panic. *Stay calm,* she told herself as she finished gathering the right bills. *You aren't doing anything wrong.*

She nodded glumly. "Our father died recently and we were sent to live with our aunt," she replied, handing over the wad of coupons.

The woman shook her head and grunted, a gesture Liza interpreted as a rough, shortened form of sympathy. Surely the woman wouldn't gush at such a sad story since everyone she met had a similar one. Besides, even before the virus she probably hadn't been much of a gusher.

By the time Liza had repacked the sack and headed to the exit, Keely was there, waiting for her with the milk.

"Let me see what you got," she said as they hit the sidewalk.

Liza opened the bag and Keely peered inside.

"This is all great!" Keely exclaimed. "I'm so glad you thought about the first aid kit. I'd totally blanked on that."

Liza smiled proudly. Maybe she could do this after all. She didn't need a guy to lead her around. She could be strong and independent. Just like Keely.

FORTY-FOUR

DIEGO WAS TIRED OF ARGUING WITH MICHAEL. "THIS IS A BIG mistake."

"So you've said," Michael grumbled. "Seven times already."

Diego folded his arms. "Well, it's true. We have no business running right to the authorities," he muttered, tossing a pebble into the empty, stained fountain they were sitting on. "And you should know that. Aren't you a wanted fugitive?"

"Yeah," Michael said with a sigh. "That's why I'm here spending my morning with you instead of scouting with the girls. Lucky me."

Diego frowned. The guy could be such a frat boy at times. Diego could have gone off with the girls. Instead he'd decided to stay behind and work on Michael, trying to get him to see the light.

He looked out over the plaza, the one place they'd found where people seemed to be allowed to congregate. Since it was bordered by both a health clinic and a voucher bank and both places were always insanely busy, people had been granted the right to spill out onto the square. Of course, there were also about half a dozen armed soldiers pacing the perimeter. Each one had a rifle, a walkie-talkie, and a cold, wary gaze. Diego watched them closely, feeling his old, familiar dread.

Otherwise he felt especially good—better than he had in weeks. Mending things with Irene seemed to have mended him as well. He was more relaxed, more sober. And he no longer felt the need to run away.

Still, if he was sticking around, he was going to be the sole voice of reason in this outfit.

"I still can't believe you think we can trust these people," he said, keeping his eye on the nearest guard.

Michael grunted in exasperation and lay down on the concrete rim of the fountain, cushioning his head with his hands. "Please. Not again."

"Seriously, Michael. I know you guys think we can find someone who will help us, but that's ridiculous. We can't depend on anyone, no matter how nice they seem."

"I disagree," Michael said with a shrug. "I knew a lot of soldiers who were good guys in New York. It was how I survived."

"But this is different," Diego muttered, shaking his head. "This could get us thrown in jail. Or worse."

Michael sat up and stared at Diego grimly. "Look, I understand how leery you must be after getting shot, but you have to realize those guys aren't all bad. Like the guy on the street yesterday. You just have to know who to trust."

"It's not so much the people that I distrust," Diego mumbled, focusing on a soldier's AK-47 glinting in the Texas sun. "It's the system they work for."

Michael nudged Diego's shoulder and pointed across the mall's weedy expanse. "Here come the girls."

Keely, Irene, and Liza strolled up to the fountain. They looked tired and flushed. Diego caught Irene's eye, and the two of them exchanged small, private smiles.

"What did you find out?" Michael asked.

"Plenty," Irene replied in a whisper. "We talked to several people along Crawford Street and they all seem pretty happy with this guy Colonel Garrison and his platoon. Apparently he let a lot of the shops on the south side stay there rather than relocating them to the more central streets."

Diego scowled. "But are you sure we can trust him?"

"They spoke pretty highly of him," Keely said. "They say he's kept the city really safe and well supplied but that he's also really fair when it comes to dealing with problems."

"And it wasn't just one or two people saying this, but almost everyone we talked to," Liza added.

Michael rose to his feet. "I say we go see him now.

The sooner we tell them about Novo Mundum, the sooner they can plan a way to help those people."

"I agree," Keely said.

Liza and Irene nodded their approval. Everyone looked at Diego.

He shook his head and heaved a noisy sigh. "I'll say it one last time. This could be a major mistake. Once we go spill our story, there's no turning back." He glanced at their faces, searching for any signs of trepidation, but there were none.

"Fine," he said, walking up beside Irene. "I'll go too."

They headed down the block in their usual pattern—Diego and Irene first, followed by Michael, Liza, and Keely—spacing themselves out so that they wouldn't draw as much attention. Diego held Irene's hand.

As they rounded the next corner, they were surprised to see a fairly sizable crowd standing around a storefront window.

"What's all that about?" Irene asked.

"I don't know." Diego frowned. Something big had to be up since this was definitely a nonregulation gathering. "Let's try to find out."

They elbowed their way into the crowd, Keely, Michael, and Liza coming in behind them. As they moved closer, they could see that the people were all huddled around a wall of TV screens. Each one showed images of giant red flames and plumes of black smoke in an otherwise idyllic forest setting. Diego strained to listen to the announcer.

". . . confirmed that approximately an hour ago, a

unit of government troops bombed a remote society in the heart of the Big Empty. So far there have been no reports of any renegades taken alive. . . ."

"Oh my God. Is that . . . ?" Irene stopped, clasping her hand to her mouth.

They all exchanged horrified glances, each one silently finishing her thought.

Novo Mundum?

FORTY-FIVE

KEELY'S HEART SEEMED TO STOP IN HER CHEST. SHE STARED IN disbelief at the images flickering in front of her. A curving road with flaming buildings on either side. In the middle an abandoned shoe and something that resembled a broken, twisted bicycle.

Did she know that street? With all the smoke and shaky camera work, she couldn't be sure.

Amber . . . Jonah . . . the kids! Keely ached as she pictured the faces of her friends and small charges. Judging by the pictures, she didn't think it possible that anyone could have survived such an assault.

She glanced around at the others' stricken faces. Irene had buried her face in Diego's chest, and both Diego and Michael appeared frozen in shock. Liza stood off to the side, staring fixedly at the television sets. Her face was whiter than white and as Keely watched, she seemed to sway slightly, like a tree in a breeze.

"Liza!" Keely quickly reached out and gripped her by the arm.

Liza turned toward her and blinked rapidly, her eyes glazed and far away. "I'm . . . okay," she said in a small, flat voice.

The crowd gasped in unison and Keely glanced back at the nearest screen. Something else had exploded in the distance, sending up a tower of smoke and flame.

Suddenly the shot blinked away, changing to an image of a young female reporter sitting calmly behind a desk. "According to official reports, the offensive was launched in an effort to protect the country from a breach of security posed by these Colorado rebels," the reporter stated smoothly.

A breach of security? Right. This was, after all, the government broadcasting channel, which was how all news was reported now in the country.

Keely leaned forward, suddenly processing the location the reporter had named. "Colorado?" she repeated. "Did she say Colorado?"

A few people nodded. Others shushed her. She turned and met Liza's eye.

"So it's not—" Liza said.

"Right," Keely said, cutting her off. She exhaled in relief. So it wasn't Novo Mundum after all.

"The society called itself the Red Haven," the reporter continued, "and its members repeatedly resisted government requests to relocate. President MacCauley released a statement calling the community 'a divisive network of terrorists bent on thwarting our efforts to rebuild our great country.'"

Red Haven? Keely remembered hearing something about them at Novo Mundum. Supposedly it was a peace-loving society, the same way Novo Mundum touted itself. Just a group of people who refused to move and live under military rule.

"As you can see," the reporter said, "the government had no choice but to use drastic methods after the radicals refused to cooperate in any peaceful negotiations."

"No choice," Diego muttered sarcastically. A woman stared at him, appalled.

"No government casualties have been reported so far, and it is unknown how many Red Haven members have been killed in the attack. However, the president has firmly denied that any children were among the dead."

Keely shuddered. Just the fact that they would announce that made it seem like they were hiding something. And bombs didn't discriminate by age.

A shrill whistle cut through the air. "All right, move along!" barked a loud, stern voice.

Keely looked around to find three soldiers walking toward the crowd, waving their arms in long, forward motions. "Come on! Break it up!" People immediately began to hurry off in different directions.

"This way," Michael said, gesturing with his head.

They followed him for a couple of blocks until they came to a courtyard in front of a tall, deserted office building.

"What do we do now?" Liza asked as they huddled at the foot of a statue.

"Well, we certainly can't go to any authorities like we planned," Michael said. "Diego was right. We can't trust them."

"That's for sure," Irene said. "They'd probably end up bombing everyone in Novo Mundum."

"We came all this way for nothing," Diego muttered, slumping against the statue.

"So what now?" Liza asked again.

"We can't give up," Michael said. "There may not be anyone out there we can trust, but we still have each other. And we've got to stick together."

"Like family," Irene added.

Family . . . Something stirred in the back of Keely's mind. She remembered what Jane had told her or at least hinted at. If it were true, then what she was thinking right now could be the perfect solution. It could be that they already knew the one person who could actually help, someone who would never, ever be a part of the wholesale destruction of an entire community no matter what but who just might have the knowledge and connections to stop Dr. Slattery another way.

Keely glanced up and down the avenue and spotted a call center set up in the remains of an Italian restaurant. "Listen, guys," she said quickly. "I might have another way. Does anyone have vouchers on them?"

"Here," Irene said, thrusting a wad of folded notes in her hands. "What are you thinking of?"

"Just a phone call." Clutching the stack of coupons, Keely jogged across the road and stepped inside the call center. It was relatively empty: only a couple of people sat among the vast bank of phones. A white-haired woman stood up from behind a desk near the entrance. "Can I help you?" she asked.

"I'd like to buy a fifteen-minute call," Keely said, counting out several of their valuable coupons. God, she hoped this wasn't a total waste.

Settling herself at a phone near the back, she took a deep breath and punched out the familiar string of numbers. Her heart hammered as a faint ring came over the line . . . then two rings . . . three. . . .

Suddenly she heard a click followed by a woman's weary voice. "Hello?"

"Hi, Mom? It's me, Keely."